MW01104008

Love According to Teresa

To Ruth,

a fellow penwoman. Best wishes,

Florence Boutwell

1-24-02

Love According to Teresa

by
Florence Boutwell

Cover and illustrations by
Janet Ivie

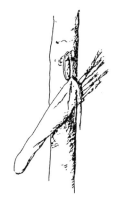

MILLWOOD PUBLISHING
Spokane, Washington
2000

Other Books by Florence Boutwell

The Spokane Valley, A History of the Early Years
The Spokane Valley, A History of the Growing Years
The Spokane Valley, Out in the Gravel
Teresa of Northwood Prairie
Teresa and the Coeur d'Alene Indians

First Edition

Copyright 2000 by
FLORENCE BOUTWELL

Millwood Publishing
is a division of
The Arthur H. Clark Company
P.O. Box 14707
Spokane, WA 99214

LIBRARY OF CONGRESS CATALOG CARD NUMBER 99-89760
ISBN-0-87062-298-6

Contents

This book is a novel based on local Spokane Valley history. The Mullan Road, Plante's Ferry, Trent, the Spokane River and Spokane Falls existed at the time of this story (1887) and exist today (1999) although Spokane Falls is now called Spokane and parts of the path of the Mullan Road have become I-90.

The characters are all fictitious except for Mr. Cowley, the proprietor of the store at Spokane Bridge, and Rosa McMahan, County Superintendent of Schools. Historically, there were persons with those names in those jobs at the time of the story. However, due to a lack of available specifics about them, their characters and dialogue in the story are imaginary.

Northwood Prairie is so completely imaginary that except for the Mullan Road, it has been located on roads and trails that, to my knowledge, never existed.

Foreword

A brief look at
Book 1, *Teresa of Northwood Prairie*
Book 2, *Teresa and the Coeur d'Alene Indians*
Book 3, *Love According to Teresa*

All four books of this series are told in first person by fictitious Teresa Wickstrom after she is grown and married. The setting is the Spokane River Valley from Spokane Falls to Coeur d'Alene.

Book 1: The year is 1886. Papa Wickstrom has died. Mama brings the children — Teresa, Thad, Henry, Emmy — from New York City to homestead near Uncle Ray and Aunt May in Washington Territory.

Villainous Ferguson Fenrich plots to take the Wickstrom's cabin and land. Thad and Teresa with Nature Boy, Wild Willie, save the day at an hilarious Fourth of July celebration.

Book 2: (1887) Teresa and Thad, with Steve Liberty, Coeur d'Alene Indian Chief, Joseph Seltice, and Spokane Falls Marshal, Joel Warren, are caught up in adventure while trying to help solve the murder of a would-be miner and the Coeur d'Alene Indian reservation boundary dispute.

Book 3: Teresa and Thad, who are eighth-graders when they come west, are home-schooled on the prairie. They long for a "real" school.

On February 15, 1999, a photo taken in 1933 of a pioneer schoolhouse located about one mile north of Trentwood appeared in the *Spokesman-Review.*

In my mind I had always located Northwood Prairie in the hills of Trentwood. Was this the sort of "real" school Thad and Teresa would have attended, had there been a school for them? Would they have liked it? How would the school have come about?

These are the questions Book 3 answers as Thad and Teresa solve the mystery of a mixed-up map and mysterious roof. Meanwhile, Teresa learns about "love" when she can not interest her best friend, Luke Aaron, in school — but he is anxious to help the pretty Sarah Stebbins' parents organize a school.

CHAPTER 1

A Happening at Spokane Bridge

I FINISHED MY SHOPPING at the Spokane Bridge store.

Proprietor Cowley, helpful as usual, carried out the fifty-pound bag of flour I had bought and hoisted it into my cart.

I was placing my other groceries near the flour when a team and wagon drove up beside me. In the wagon bed were four red-haired boys and one auburn-haired girl.

"What's the toll to cross the bridge?" the blond man driving the team called.

"Four dollars for the team and wagon," I answered. "Might be more for the passengers. I'm not sure. I've never been across the bridge."

"Father, I'll go in and ask," the tallest of the four boys said.

He stood up, put his hand on the side rail of the wagon bed and prepared to swing out.

At that moment the team snorted and momentarily jerked the wagon.

The boy lost his balance and landed next to me, knocking a sack of assorted groceries out of my hand.

The other boys jumped up, scrambling to help pick up the groceries.

9

"Get back in," the father said. "Axtel can take care of this himself."

"I'm sorry I was clumsy," the boy said to me, and his gray-blue eyes smiled. "I'm Axtel Stebbins."

CHAPTER 2

A Happening at the Spokane River

THAD AND I HAD been working all day in the hot May sun grubbing out roots to add space to our garden area.

Tired and dirty, Thad said, "Tress, let's take a dip in the river before supper."

"Let's," I said, wiping the sweat from my forehead onto the sleeve of my work shirt.

"Papa Willie," Thad called to a middle-aged man working nearby, "Tress and I are going to take a dip in the river before supper. Will you tell Mama?"

"Stay in the cove we fixed for swimming. No going out into the current. The river's tricky this time of year," Papa Willie warned us. "And don't stay too long. We'll wait supper for you."

We trudged to the house, changed quickly into swimming suits Mama had made us and put our work clothes on over them so the brush wouldn't scratch us on the way. We found our walking sticks where we had left them in the crook of the apple tree in front of our house and started off down our trail.

Although too tired to hurry, we soon crossed the Mullan Road, passed the rock we called Resting Rock, and didn't stop until we came to the river.

Even hotter and sweatier now, we slipped out of our work clothes and dove right in. Oh joy! Cold, cold water. I came up for air , then ducked my head under again.

In the channel, the water swirled and foamed. Now and then I felt the tug of the current on my foot as I swam a little farther out than I should have. How refreshing the crystal clear water was! I floated on the surface, dove under a ripple, and imagined I was one of the fish that lazed in the shallow.

Thad and I knew the bottom well all the way across the river. When the water was low last fall, we had waded to the other side and ventured short distances along the shore, always talking of some-day exploring the south side of the river.

"Look! Up at the bend," Thad called, swimming over to me.

A boat with one rider tipped and careened crazily toward us. A man, slightly built, struggled to row; but each time he brought the oar toward his body, the current lurched it from his grasp.

"He's not able to steer at all," Thad said.

"No wonder. Look how he's dressed. He can't move his neck in that starched white collar and bow tie. Can you imagine anyone rowing in a flow-ered vest and dress pants on a hot day like today?"

"He's caught in the current. He can't control the oars. He's giving up, letting his row boat bump along with the flow. We better get out of the water 'till he gets past. What's that lying in the stern?"

"Something wrapped in oil cloth. I wonder where he's headed," I said.

"I wonder if he knows there's a falls farther on."

"He's looking this way. I'm going to climb on that rock so he'll see me."

From my viewpoint on the rock, dangling my feet in the water, I waved and yelled.

As the boat bounced nearer, I called louder, "Hello-o-o!" and waved wildly.

Standing in knee deep water, Thad cupped his hands to his mouth and yelled as loud as he could, "Get your boat out of the current."

The man stood up unsteadily and tried to wave to us. The boat rocked, swerved.

"Sit down. You'll capsize."

He tried to steady himself. He lost his balance. The prow rose high out of the water. He flipped out head first and disappeared under the foam.

13

"C'mon, Tress," Thad yelled, starting to swim. "Maybe he's hurt. We've got to get him."

The man surfaced gasping, his arms thrashing about.

We swam toward him.

"It isn't over your head there. Try to stand up before you get caught in the current," Thad called.

He grabbed for the branch of a spindly overhanging tree. He pulled himself upright just as the branch snapped in his hand. He fell back into the water.

"Are you all right?" Thad yelled wading toward him.

"Thought it was deeper than it is," the man sputtered standing up, wet and dripping. "Never was much of a swimmer or boatman, but I thought I could handle that little boat. Didn't allow for the strong current."

He waded toward the boat now upended and lodged against a rock near the shore.

"The map. My map is gone," he moaned, staring at the empty boat. He looked around, even put his face in the water for a minute as though trying to see the bottom of the river where he stood. He looked again toward the swirling current; then with effort and dripping, he climbed out of the water onto our beach.

He looked ruefully at his soggy vest, white shirt and pants. His clinging clothes exaggerated his lean build. He tried to slick his neatly trimmed, short black water-soaked hair close to his head.

"I made a special trip to the Bridge to get that map," he said. "I have a client who needs it in a hurry. From Chicago, going back on today's train. I'll never get it to him in time now."

"You shouldn't have tried to row in the middle of the river," Thad said. "The water's high from mountain run-off this time of the year."

"Never rowed before. A fellow at the Bridge loaned me his boat when my horse became lame. Knew I was in a hurry. Told me to leave my horse there and take his boat and he would bring my horse and get his boat tomorrow. Wrapped my map in oil cloth so it wouldn't get wet and pushed me off. Got along fine until I hit the rapids."

Again he stared helplessly at the boat.

Thad and I righted it and dragged it to shore.

He followed, stumbling through the water, still looking for the map.

"My trip was for nothing. Without that map, my deal is washed up."

"Your map could be over the Falls by now," Thad said.

"But if you should by some lucky chance find it while you're swimming, would you save it for me? I'm Elliot Vandersims, Dealer in Land. I'm developing a piece of property down Plante's Ferry way."

"I'm Thad Wickstrom. This is my twin sister, Teresa. I call her Tress. If we should find your map, don't worry, we'll save it for you. Will you be this way again soon?"

"Should be. I have more business with the map maker at the Bridge. Where do you live?"

"Up the hill across the Mullan Road. Our sign is on a tree there."

Elliot Vandersims squeezed water out of his pantlegs, took off his soppy vest, put it on the seat of the boat and climbed in.

"At least the oars are still in the oarlocks," he said.

Thad pushed the boat off.

"You're lucky we were here and you didn't drown," he said. "Keep the boat near shore this time."

Standing unsteadily, Mr. Vandersims polled the boat along in the shallow with one oar, digging it into the river bottom. Now and then scraping the bottom, the boat alternately jerked and floated, weaving down the river and disappearing around the bend.

"I'll bet he doesn't make it as far as Plante's Ferry," Thad said.

"He'll fall in, for sure, before he gets there," I agreed.

I waded into the water, held my nose and bent backward to wet my hair and get it out of my eyes.

"Thad! I think I see his map. Lodged against that rock."

Thad swam toward the oil cloth wrapped roll.

A wave splashed against the rock and hurled the package within easy reach. He grabbed for it and scooped it out of the water.

He took it ashore and loosened the thin leather thong strapping that held the oil cloth in place. Water had seeped into the contents. "It *is* a map!" Thad said.

He spread the soggy paper on a rock to dry while we finished our swim. Then we sat down on a nearby rock to let our suits dry before we started home.

We tried to make the map out.

"There's the railroad bridge at Trent. That circle says *warehouse*, Tress. Someone must be going to build a warehouse down Trent way. Maybe Mr. Vandersims' client. Trent is only two or three miles away. A warehouse! That means jobs. Maybe no more farming for us, Tress. I wish I knew for sure."

"Let's take the map back to Mr. Vandersims and find out."

"We don't know where he lives. Maybe he wouldn't tell us his business."

"We could start looking for him at Trent. If he deals in land, it shouldn't be hard to find him."

"Thad, to get to Trent, we would have to cross the river. There's no bridge near there. And the water's too high to cross at the ford."

"The bridge at Spokane Falls is too far away."

"The bridge at Spokane Bridge would cost toll. Mama and Papa Willie couldn't afford to let us cross there."

"If we had a boat, it would be easy."

"The only way we'll ever get a boat is to build it ourselves."

"We could. The Indians build canoes. I think I'll ask some of our Indian friends how they do it."

"We wouldn't have time until after the new part of the garden is in and the fences are built."

"What about building just a raft?"

Thad thought before he answered. "We might be

able to build that ourselves. It would be a way of getting across the river without going to Spokane Falls or Spokane Bridge."

The sun was beginning to descend in the western sky. A breeze had come up.

"We better get home," Thad said as he rolled the oil cloth around the map and tied up the package. "Supper will be over."

"Thad, let's climb the mountain after supper. From our look-out we could see if a warehouse is being built down Trent way."

"If we hurry. It's getting late. Listen to the crickets."

Walking up the hill, we talked more about Elliot Vandersims and the map and the possibility of a real job at a warehouse.

"A warehouse will bring people looking for jobs," Thad said. "More people might mean a schoolhouse – all kinds of new things. Maybe a store and a church."

Both Thad and I wanted to earn money and we wanted to go to a real school. Thad had a rock collection and hoped someday to go to college and learn to be a geologist. I had an Indian friend named Eloika. Her family worried about losing their land to white settlers. I wanted to help the Indians and talked of being an Indian agent some day. Thad reminded me again and again that "girls can't be things like that."

At Resting Rock we sat for a minute watching Mr. Vandersims now in sight farther down the river struggling with the boat.

"Thad! Look! It's still light and the evening star is up already. Make a wish."

"What did you wish, Tress?"

"For the warehouse and a real school and a boat."

"I wished for the same things!"

That was the first time I realized that Thad, in a way, was like me even though he was a boy. We had both wished for the same things.

When we reached the cabin, Mama, Papa Willie, our big brother Henry and little sister Emmy had finished supper.

"What's that?" Emmy asked pointing to the map Thad carried.

"It's a map. We fished it out of the river," I said and told them about the boat and Elliot Vandersims, Dealer in Land.

Papa was excited. He spread the damp map out on the table.

"Look at this, Addy," he said. "Here's the Spokane River. Wouldn't you say this is a map of the area across the river not far from Plante's Ferry called Trent?"

"That dotted line is the railroad bridge."

"I'd bet a Silver Eagle this here is a plat map," Papa Willie said. "Didn't you say Elliot Vandersims was a dealer in land?"

"He said he was."

"We'd best keep this map safe if he said he'd be back for it," Mama said. She laid it out on the porch to dry.

"Thad, let's us take the map to Mr. Vandersims," I said.

"Good idea."

"Why not ask your friend, Luke, to drop it off the next time he takes a load of cordwood to Spokane Falls?" Mama asked.

"I don't think he goes on that side of the river. Let's hurry with supper, Thad, so we can climb the mountain before it gets dark."

CHAPTER 3

Axtel Stebbins

THE WINTER DAYS of ice and snow had melted away at Northwood Prairie. Each day the sun seemed to shine brighter and more green shoots popped through dead stubble. The yard around our cabin was yellow with dog tooth violets.

It was the time of year when Thad and I followed new trails and climbed up into the hills as often as we could. We watched the Spokane River far below, wild with spring run-off. Next year we would know exactly when to expect the ocean spray, wild cherry, elderberry and serviceberry to bloom along its banks.

We kept track of population changes. Wherever we saw clusters of roofs, we imagined a store, a train depot, a church and a school. How we wished for a school, but it would have to be on our side of the river if we were to go.

We had crossed the river at Spokane Falls a few times on errands, but we had never been beyond the city limits and had never crossed at Spokane Bridge. We yearned to explore over there. The scattered new buildings that we spied seemed always to be across the river – never on our side.

When we told Mama how we longed for the companionship a school and church would bring, she promised, "When enough settlers come on our side, there will be a school and a church. The settlers will get together and build a building that can be used for both and we will petition the Territorial Government for school money."

So we waited and watched the Spokane Valley grow, always at Spokane Falls or across the river. Always out of our reach.

*   *   *   *

In addition to wanting a school and a church, Henry, Thad and I wanted a job other than farming. Farming was not in our blood. We had lived too long in the hustle and bustle of New York City.

Thad and I ate as fast as we could, excused ourselves and hurried to our stream to fill our canteens with water.

"We've got about three hours until it will be coal dark," I said. "I'll go get the map. Are you ready, Thad?"

"Just need to get my machete. Wait a minute, Tress! I think I hear wagon wheels on the back trail."

"It's Luke. What's he doing here this time of day?"

Luke Aaron lived on the homestead next to ours. His father was a carpenter and Luke sold firewood in Spokane Falls. One day last winter he and another friend and Thad and I saved Eddie Chuck, a half breed Indian in trouble with the law, from being hanged. After that, Luke and I became good friends. With our farm work and Luke's cutting wood, neither of us had much extra time, but I cherished every minute I spent with him.

There wasn't water on his parents' property so he often drove his team to our spring to fill his water barrels. I was glad. Whenever I heard the rumble of his wagon on the back trail, I dropped whatever I was doing and ran out to meet him. He was the only friend I had on the prairie who was near my age. His pa had plans to dig a well, but I hoped it never happened. I liked Luke coming for water.

"Want to go for a hike?" he called.

We helped him tether his horses in the tender spring grass near our stream.

"Ma says there's been somebody snooping around. She wants me to look around in the forest and see if it looks like strangers is camping nearby."

"You're just in time. We're getting ready to go to the rock outcropping. Come with us."

"Perfect," Luke said. "Could be the snooper is hiding out on the mountain."

"Henry's seen someone snooping around, too. I'm taking my machete," Thad said. "It will be protection. Tress and I always take it to cut away brush. We've hacked out a good trail with it."

"Luke, we've got a map that shows a warehouse at Trent," I said. "We're hoping the map is right. A warehouse might mean jobs for Tress and me and Henry or even Papa Willie. Did you hear anything about a warehouse when you took your last load of cordwood to Spokane Falls? Seems like if a warehouse is planned or started at Trent, people would be talking about it."

"Trent's on the other side of the river. There's

lots of folks never cross the river. I never go that way."

"Let's get going," Thad said. "We can talk as we climb. Mama wants us home before dark."

We struck off on the back trail that headed up the mountain.

"Keep a sharp look out for the snooper," Luke said. "Ma will rest easier if I can tell her whose footprints she saw in our back pasture."

We heard animal and bird noises in the brush, but that was all. Papa Willie had taught us the names of the wild life and we liked showing off our knowledge, but Luke did not seem interested. His interest was in the timber.

"Pa wants me to learn all I can about timber," he said. "He's teaching me his carpenter trade. He probably wouldn't let me work in the warehouse if there is one. He likes me selling wood."

About halfway up, we came to the stream that eventually watered our property. "We call this the deer stream," I told Luke. "The first time we came up here, we saw a mother deer and her fawn drinking."

Using our hands for a cup, we drank from it.

"Sure would like to find some way to bring water to our property," Luke said.

"I'm going to dig a ditch from our stream to our new garden to water it," Thad said. "Carrying water for our little garden last summer was a big job."

"I hear that some of the new settlers in the valley across the river are digging wells," Luke said. "Pa and I've been thinking about a well for our spread."

For the better part of an hour, we went on up through thick stands of pine and spruce and hemlock, but saw no suspicious footprints and heard no unusual noises. We let Luke take a turn at clearing the path with the machete. He swung it like the woodsman he was — like somebody who was used to swinging an ax.

"I'd like to file a timber claim up here when I'm eighteen," he said. "Who owns all this land?"

"We don't know," Thad said. "Could be the Coeur d'Alene Indians."

"I'm going to tell my pa about this. He says he'd like to get me some more land to log off."

"Mama wants land to run cattle on," I said.

When we reached the rock outcropping, we were high above the trees. Eagles soared gracefully about, sometimes floating along over the treetops and sometimes swooping far down to the river below.

Thad unrolled the map and settled himself on a rock to study it.

"Tress," Luke said. "Down there. On that rock a little to the right of us. There's someone down there."

"There is! Thad, come here." I said as quietly as I could.

"I see him," Thad said.

"Not hard to see that red hair with the sun on it. Whoever it is, isn't trying to hide."

"I think he's the person I met at the Bridge!" I exclaimed.

Luke scuffed a pile of rocks down the mountainside, starting them tumbling noisily.

"Hello, up there," the red-headed boy called.

"What are you doing here?" Thad answered.

"Stay there. I'll come up."

We watched him start up the trail. He soon disappeared in the trees.

"Luke, do you really think he'll come?" I asked.

"Depends on what he's doing up here."

"Luke, Tress, come over here while we're waiting. Look at this map. Now look down toward the railroad bridge. What do you see?"

"Down near Plante's Ferry, I see the new saloon and boarding house and the remains of the old saloon. Oh, I see what you mean. Near the railroad bridge I see a roof that I've never noticed there before," I said.

"Exactly," Thad answered. "And it seems to be at the spot where this map of Mr. Vandersims shows a warehouse. That roof doesn't look big enough to be a warehouse."

We puzzled about the roof, thought we had waited long enough for the red-haired boy and were about to start down when we heard, "Yo – o o," and the red-haired boy came into view.

"Hurried as fast as I could," the boy said. "When you saw me, I was on my way down. Say," he looked at me. "You're the girl whose groceries I spilled!"

The gray-blue eyes smiled at me.

"And you're the person who picked them up. Axtel, wasn't it?"

"Axtel Stebbins," he said.

I introduced Thad and Luke and showed Axtel Mr. Vandersims' map. Then I pointed out the roof and told him we hoped it was the beginnings of the warehouse but thought it looked too small.

"You're right. It's no warehouse. That roof is our house. You won't believe this. I was up here drawing a map of the area for Father."

He pulled a piece of brown paper from his overalls pocket.

Thad studied Axtel's map, then Mr. Vandersims' map. He looked up. "Why would anyone make a map that shows a warehouse on property where a house already stands?"

"You don't have to go to school to figure that out," Luke said. "Somebody's decided the house won't be there long."

"How could that be? My father has no plans to sell." The boy's face sobered. "Or if he has, he didn't tell me."

"Is anything wrong, Axtel?" I asked.

"I hope not. I'd best not say any more. My father doesn't like us to talk about his affairs."

We stared at Axtel. He looked worried. Thad broke the silence.

"Tress, we've just got to get this map back to Mr. Vandersims and ask him some questions."

"This Saturday I'm taking a load of cordwood to the Falls," Luke said. "Why don't you two come with me? We will cross the river at Spokane Falls. When the wood is all sold, we will work our way to Trent on the south side of the river."

"I don't know," Thad said. "To get back across, we'd have to go all the way to Spokane Bridge and that costs toll."

"Besides, Papa Willie might have work lined up for us this week-end," I said.

"Let's get started back down the mountain and find out," Luke said. "I almost forgot. . ." He turned to Axtel Stebbins. "You didn't happen to see any-body suspicious-looking along the trail, did you?"

Axtel smiled, "Only you three."

"Luke's ma said someone's been nosing around their place."

"Could have been me. I had trouble finding the entrance to this path up the hill."

Going down was quicker than coming up even though we stopped to kick rocks and listen as they rolled and tumbled far below.

At the bottom of the trail Axtel went on to the Mullan Road. Thad ran ahead to the house.

"Tress," Luke said. "If your ma and pa won't let you go with me on Saturday, some day let's you and me take Charlie and the cart to Trent. We could tie Charlie on the north side then you and me could cross the river on the railroad bridge."

"Papa Willie wouldn't let me walk across on the railroad bridge. Thad and I have asked to do that before."

"We wouldn't have to tell nobody."

CHAPTER 4

Eddie Chuck

I WAS RIGHT: Papa Willie and Mama said they couldn't spare us until the new garden work was finished.

I thought a lot about the sad look on Axtel Stebbins' otherwise smiling face and the mixed up maps.

And I thought about Luke suggesting that he and I get Charlie and the cart and go to Trent alone and walk across the river on the railroad bridge.

Time spent with Luke was special to me and I usually jumped at the chance to be with him. But I didn't like doing something I had been told not to do and I didn't like not telling Mama and Papa Willie where I was going. They had impressed upon us the danger of going off by ourselves.

One morning as the sun streamed in my bedroom window and I lay half asleep wondering when Thad and I could take the map back to Mr. Vandersims, I was jolted wide awake by the opening and closing of the front door.

A man's voice called, "Rise and shine. There's work to get to."

It was our new Papa Willie's voice. Although he and Mama had been married recently by the horseback preacher, he still lived at his own cabin with his animals until he finished building a new bedroom onto our house for himself and Mama. He came early every morning to begin that work. But not usually this early!

The "work" he wanted us to "get to" was grub hoeing roots out of virgin soil to enlarge our garden. With more garden, Mama planned that Thad and I would sell the extra produce to the hotels in Spokane Falls.

Our real papa's life insurance money had lasted through the winter. Now it was running out. "High time we began to fend for ourselves. High time we earned our keep," Mama said.

At Papa Willie's call, the cabin came alive. We had learned the hard way that it was best to heed the wake-up call. One hot day we hadn't come when called and had to do our chores later in the blazing sun. Once was enough.

Thad and I scrambled into our work clothes. In no time we were out getting our garden tools from the lean-to barn.

Even seven-year-old Emmy needed no prodding. She, too, was into her overalls and following Thad and me.

I was sorry for Emmy. She worked along with us all day, then studied along with us after the lamp was lighted in the evening. On week ends she played outside — alone unless she again trailed along with Thad and me when we went fishing or hiking.

She had no playmates her own age. I remembered going happily to real school in New York City when I was her age.

I wished she had a school to go to.

I was surprised to see Mama kindling a fire in the outside fire pit. That meant breakfast outside — "to celebrate our first breakfast on the prairie," she said. "Do you realize it was just one year ago today that Uncle Ray brought us, bag and baggage, to the prairie?"

When I saw Henry lugging a big black kettle from the barn for Mama, I knew there was another reason we were having breakfast outside. After breakfast the fire in the pit would be used for soap-making. Into the kettle would go fat and lye. Mama would stir and boil enough soap mixture to last us through the winter.

As I sat on a log eating my hot cakes, I heard, "Hello, you Wickstroms."

It was my Indian friend, Eloika.

I set down my plate and ran to the top of the road that led from the Mullan Road up our hill.

There was someone with Eloika! A rider on a crippled brown saddle horse.

I called to the others, "It's Eloika and. . ."

I stared. It couldn't be! But it was. Eddie Chuck!

Why was Eloika bringing him of all people to our home? Eloika was my trusted friend. She had been my very first friend here on the prairie — except for Lucky, my dog.

"Hello, you Wickstroms," Eloika said again. "I can see you're surprised to see Eddie and me so early. I told Eddie, 'Don't worry about going too early. On a sunny morning like this the Wickstroms will be up and working at sun-up.' Eddie and I have a favor to ask."

Eddie! a *favor* to ask of *us*? Eddie was the part Indian we had saved from being wrongfully hanged. He had painted his face black to hide small pox scars and had gotten into trouble with the law.

Mama, Emmy, Henry, Thad and I were too surprised to speak.

Papa Willie set down his coffee mug and walked over to Eloika and Eddie. A hammer and a screwdriver peeped out of the side pocket of his overalls. When we first met him a year ago at the Spokane River, he wore only cut-off overalls. He began dressing normally at the cabin moving when he started courting Mama.

"You and Eddie get off those horses and join us for breakfast," Papa Willie said.

Eloika slid off her pinto. "Help me out, Willie," she said. "Tell them why I brought Eddie Chuck along."

"Eloika, if I'm to tell why Eddie Chuck is visiting us this morning, seems to me I'd best tell the whole story from beginning to end. You and Eddie help yourself to some of Addy's side pork and hot cakes."

Papa said to us, "All you Wickstroms, move the logs you're setting on back away from the fire some, so's you don't get your whiskers singed. Teresa Girl, make sure everybody has all the breakfast they need and that everybody's set to hear a story."

"William, this is a busy morning," Mama said. "Make this a short story, please."

"No worry, Addy. You can go on with your soap making soon as all has had all the breakfast they want. But you young'uns, best to give me your un-de-vided attention. We'll need a vote of the clan after you hear what me and Eloika cooked up one day at the Bridge."

"What's a vote of the clan?" Emmy asked.

"You'll see," Papa Willie said. "For Henry and Emmy and me new wife, Addy here, who's never met this fellow on the crippled horse, I'll say first off, this here is Eddie Chuck. Thad and Teresa have already had dealings with him."

When I saved Eddie Chuck from being hanged and he said to me, "Nika mica tillucum" which in Chinook means *we are friends*, I never expected Eddie to visit us here on Northwood Prairie.

I was puzzled. What were Eloika and Papa Willie planning?

The sun had already warmed our arms and faces. We gladly moved our logs as far from the fire as we could get and still hear.

Papa Willie said, "I'll come to the point right off. Eddie Chuck needs a job so's he can live like a decent human being and not be running wild and accused of every dad-blasted crime that comes up.

Eloika explained all that to me when I was at the Bridge yesterday.

"I said to myself, I said, 'William Webster Whitehouse, giving Eddie a job at your diggin's would take some of the burden of keeping this homestead on course off the shoulders of Addy, your new wife. She needs someone to give her a hand on this here spread."

Eddie Chuck? Give Mama a hand?

"Eloika says Eddie Chuck's sworn to Chief Seltice to stay away from fire water. Marshal Warren of Spokane Falls and Chief Seltice laid down the law to Eddie. He's got to find honest work with folks who needs him and knows about him. That's us. Eddie knows he wouldn't be here today if Teresa Girl hadn't saved him from hanging."

"Well, I never," Mama said, her favorite expression when she was surprised or startled.

"Having Eddie to do some of the heavy work will take a load off you and me, Addy, and the young'uns," Papa Willie said.

"Would be a help," Mama agreed.

"Eddie's ready to start a new life and he'll show us he's ready by cleaning up his face," Papa Willie said. "So's folks won't be scared out of a year's growth when they come acrost him."

Eddie Chuck, sitting next to Eloika and enjoying a plate of Mama's hot cakes, nodded. His face was still painted black.

"Well, what do you say? Do you want an extra hand or not?"

34

Silence. Then Thad said, "I could sell fire wood in Spokane Falls like Luke does if I had someone to help me cut the timber."

"Mighty fine thinkin'," Papa Willie said.

"Will he live with us?" Emmy asked.

"A hired man living with us would be a help." Henry said.

"But how could we pay him?" Mama asked.

"Room and board is all he's asking," Papa Willie answered.

"Where will he bunk?"

"We'll be needing a new barn when I move in so's I can bring my cow and Mabel, my horse. You Wickstroms will need space for your new team when your Uncle Ray brings it," Papa Willie said. "Eddie can have the old lean-to barn to fix up for hisself. I'd be willing to bet a Silver Eagle that Eddie Chuck will be a help around here."

"William, you know I don't like betting," Mama said.

"You folks talk it over," Eloika said, "I've got to get back and help Mama Anna. We're getting ready to put in our garden, too. I'll leave Eddie with you today and you can try him out. How about taking Teresa's grub hoe, Eddie, and showing the Wickstroms what you can do."

I had left my grub hoe standing against the house. I ran over, picked it up and handed it gladly to Eddie Chuck. Then I led him to the unbroken sod near the garden where Thad, Emmy and I had been working.

Eddie Chuck, like many Coeur d'Alene Indian men, was about 5'6" tall but strong. Living in the cave at the Devil's Underjaw and hiding in the forest during the winter had toughened him.

He nodded to me and said, "Nika mika tillucum," and went right to work.

"Why, I haven't said he could stay," Mama said.

"You won't be sorry, Addy," Papa Willie said. "You'll need all the help you can get this spring. There's a new barn to be built, and fences to put up, and extra garden to tend. We'll need an extra hand. I'll see that Eddie's face is cleaned up and you'll be mighty glad he's here. But just to make sure we're all agreed to this, tomorrow we'll have the meeting of the clan and vote on it."

"Papa Willie, you didn't tell us what a meeting of the clan is," Emmy said.

"You'll see. Be out here at the pit at daybreak tomorrow."

CHAPTER 5

The Meeting of the Clan

T HAD AND I WERE all for keeping Eddie Chuck. We thought an extra hand might mean we would have some free time to explore the south side of the river and find out what that roof was. And if it were a warehouse, with Eddie doing some of the garden work, Mama might let Thad and me get a job there. Gardening was hard work.

When Papa Willie said *daybreak*, we found out the next morning that he meant exactly that.

I was sound asleep when I was awakened by what turned out to be a drum roll on Papa Willie's old Civil War drum and our dog Lucky yelping in what he probably thought was "in tune".

I sat up straight in bed, then ran to the front door.

Mama rushed to the door, too, in her night gown, followed by Emmy, rumpled and sleepy-eyed. "What's that? What are you doing drumming out there, William?"

"All you Wickstroms! It's daylight in the swamp. Time to be up and about. Lucky's got you all beat for getting up on time. Think you can herd the young'uns out to the fire pit this early, Addy?" Willie called. "I'm anxious to get this vote over so's me and Henry can get to working on the new room."

"I'll put the coffee pot on, William, and we'll be up before you can say 'Robinson Crusoe.'" (That was one of our real papa's sayings.)

"Breakfast will be around the fire pit again this morning, Addy. Meetings of the clan will always be at the pit."

Out to the pit we went, Mama carrying the coffee pot and I carrying the skillet. Thad and Emmy soon joined us, work clothes askew and uncombed.

"Thad, go get your Composition Book. You'll want to write down about this meetin'."

"Why does a meeting of the clan have to be so early?" Emmy asked. "What is it anyway?"

"It's a family meetin' to let the clan know that something important is about to happen — like us taking a vote on whether to keep Eddie Chuck as our hired hand," our new papa said. "And after we vote on whether to keep Eddie Chuck, I've a thing or two more to talk to you about."

"More to talk about? And why the drum, William?" Mama asked.

"Mrs. William Webster Whitehouse," Papa Willie said. "It's time to get the sour dough hot cakes baking and the side pork sizzling and let me do the worrying about what's going on in this family. It's me job now, as Papa, to keep this ship on course. We need that drum to let the hands know there's a meetin'. Thad, we'll need your harmonica, too."

We asked Papa Willie *please* to tell us what else there was to talk about.

He shook his head. "Not until we vote on Eddie Chuck," he said filling his coffee mug for the second time. "Fine May morning. The day couldn't be better for our first meetin' of the clan. Sun is coming up and I'm settin' here with a brand new family I'm mighty proud of. There's nothing that tickles a man's happy bone like the smell of coffee boiling and salt pork frying and them smells a-drifting up and over a brand new family."

Papa Willie looked at each one of us with a look that said, "I'm the luckiest man around." That look made all of us feel good: Mama and Thad and Henry and Emmy and me — and Lucky, whose stub of a tail wagged happily.

"Since there's work to be done and some is slower eating than others, I'm starting this here meeting now. Them as has big appetites can eat and listen at the same time."

We all watched as Willie set down his heaping plate on the log beside his coffee mug. He headed for his cart parked near the beginnings of the new room. From the bed of the cart, he took the drum we had already heard rolling, his old Civil War officer's cap (the one he had loaned me for the cabin moving) and a rolled up flag. He put the cap on and the straps of the drum over his shoulders, tucked the flag under his arm and hurried back to us.

"I'm a-calling this meetin' of the clan to order," he bellowed followed by a drum roll. "Keep that harmonica handy, Boy."

Papa Willie unrolled the flag — an American flag — and held it up. I counted thirty-four stars. It, like Papa's cap, must have been from the Civil War. The flag we hung out on holidays had thirty-eight stars.

"To start off this here important meetin', all stand at attention. We'll salute the grandest flag in the world."

He held it higher. With our right hands over our hearts, ". . . liberty and justice for all" reverberated from every crag.

We sang *America* with Thad playing his harmonica "to be sure the prairie critters know the name of this great land . . ."

"Now we'll say the Chinook *Our Father*," Mama cut in.

"Stay standing," Papa Willie said as Thad went for a plate.

Back in New York our real papa often had us sing when we were happy, and sometimes when we were sad to make us happy again; so this wasn't too different for us. After the "opening exercises" (as Papa Willie called the saluting), we marched around the fire pit singing some more. He and his drum and Thad and his harmonica were the leaders of the march. Lucky, as usual, trailed along behind, yelping as loud as he could. We tried to drown out our own echoes as they bounced off far away cliffs.

"Now set down," Papa Willie called.

"First off, let's get this name thing straight. You Wickstroms got yourself a new Papa but I'm not aiming to take your real papa's place and I'm not expecting you to change the name you was baptized with. So you young'uns, call me Papa Willie like you been calling me, instead of just Papa. That let's folks know you had a papa before me. You're the Wickstroms and always will be unless you want it different. Your ma, she's said she'd be pleased to be known as Mrs. William Webster Whitehouse as long as we're man and wife and I'm counting on that being till the good Lord calls me up yonder."

Mama nodded and we all clapped. She went into the house, coming out with a pitcher of Molly's cream for the coffee.

"Are you all getting the hang of what these meetin's of the clan is all about? Any morning you hear that drum roll and hear Thad playing his harmonica, it means we'll be having a meetin' and everybody's to get up lickety split and run out to the fire pit. Its just my way of keeping us all on course."

Thad looked at me and I looked at him. I didn't think we were off course, but Willie was our new papa and Mama told us, as papa, he had the right to do things his own way. She nodded her approval as Papa Willie talked. She seemed to agree with all he said, so I decided this meeting of the clan must be Willie's way of getting Mama on his side.

He told us about the new room he and Henry were adding to our cabin. And about the new barn to be built.

"Now for the vote. How do you all like the idea of having Eddie Chuck for a hired man?"

"Yesterday he grubbed out more roots than all of us put together," Henry said.

"Papa Willie," I said, "if Eddie Chuck comes to help out, could Thad and I have Saturday after-

41

noons off? We want to explore the other side of the river."

Papa Willie stroked his neatly clipped beard and thought for a moment.

"Seems fair enough if you get your chores done in the morning. You young'uns need some time to do as you dang well please. Exploring is learning and I'm all for learning. Yep, seems fair enough. Be sure to let your ma know where you go. Anything in particular you want to explore?"

"We want to find out more about that map we fished out of the river."

"Why is that so interesting?"

"If a warehouse is to be built at Trent, Tress and I want to get a job there. Also, it might be that enough people will settle there to finally have a real school."

"You two still hankering for a real school?"

"If we can find one near enough," Thad said.

Papa Willie looked as though his thoughts were far away. Then he launched into one of his stories:

"There was one time I went to a real school for a spell," he said, "when my pa was logging in the foothills of the Blue Mountains in Walla Walla county. The little old schoolhouse stood there in the mountains on a knoll.

"There was just a handful of us young'uns. One day Teacher had us all go to the water bucket an' scrub up. The county superintendent was makin' his rounds and would be visiting.

"Well, he come. There I sat, open mouthed, dangling me bare feet from an unpainted bench while Teacher presented him to us. He had letters after his name. I still remember thinking to my little self, *How does it feel to be great like that?* 'Tweren't often men with letters after their names come into the Blue Mountains.

"If you young'uns have it in mind to find a real school to go to and there's one nearby, I say give it a try. Go ahead, do your explorin.' Maybe some day you'll meet up with a county superintendent and you'll see what it's like to be great."

I couldn't believe my ears. Our new Papa Willie had not only given us permission to explore, but it sounded to me like he would do all he could to see that we got to a real school if we found one near enough.

Hoo-ray! Thad and I could get Saturday afternoons off.

Luke, if you learned anything in Spokane Falls about that "roof" hurry up and let us know. I'm ready to start exploring.

Papa Willie looked around. "I don't hear any objecting so it's decided, ain't it? Eddie Chuck is our new hired man and as soon as we get our new barn up, the lean-to is all his. 'Till then, he'll have to sleep in it as it is, with Molly and Charlie and Mabel."

"I'll run and tell Eddie," I said, still giddy from getting what I wanted so easily. "I saw him go out to the garden with the grub hoe."

"You stay here till the meetin's over, Teresa Girl. We've got more business to take up."

"More?"

"More," Willie said so definitely that I sat down. "An' there's one thing I want to add about having

Eddie Chuck here. While he's here, his name is going to be Edward Chuck, BB."

"Maybe he won't like that name. What's the BB stand for anyway?" Emmy asked.

"The BB means *Barn Boss*. Since Eddie will be living in the barn, he's got a right to be its boss," Papa Willie said. "Boss's need letters after their names the way the superintendent had who was the school boss. If Eddie's like me, there comes a time when he'll like having a dignified name. When your ma called me William instead of Willie, I knowed I was great in her all-mighty sight."

Papa Willie beamed at Mama and Emmy yawned.

He continued. "At these here meetin's, I want to give everybody a chance to say their say. Since it's spring, let's hear what the plans are for the summer, besides chores and planting the garden and helping build the new room and barn and fences and explorin' down Trent way."

CHAPTER 6

Poor Henry

"I TOLD YOU my plans, Papa Willie," Henry said. "Tomorrow I'm going to Rathdrum to see about teaching at the new school they've built there."

That was something I hadn't heard before. Our big brother Henry, whom we depended upon to be our stand-in papa might be going away to teach school! Things were certainly changing. We already had a new papa named William Webster White-house and we would soon have Edward Chuck BB and his horse, Tikut, living with us plus Willie's cow and Willie's chickens and Willie's horse Mabel and probably all the animals Willie was nursing back to health although he hadn't sprung that on us yet.

"We'll be having a lot of new animals to take care of," I said but nobody paid any attention to me.

"You young'uns can help with the new barn soon as you get the new garden plot ready," Papa Willie said.

"Is that what a meeting of the clan is for?" Thad asked. "To tell us all the work we have to do?"

"Part of it," Papa Willie said. "So's you know what's expected of you an' to help you reach goals. That's what that superintendent told us to do so long ago. 'Set goals an' reach 'em.'"

"Mama, will I still be able to go to Mama Anna for my lessons in the Chinook language?" I asked.

"Sounds like there won't be time."

"You can go now and then," Mama said. "But getting the garden in and building the barn and working on the house and fences will come first. Summer is for getting the place in shape. Schooling will start again full tilt evenings in the fall. We'll tend to first things first."

"Papa Willie, could I go to Rathdrum with Henry? Just to see what it's like over there?" Thad asked.

"Me, too?" I chimed in.

Willie lighted his corn cob pipe. "As I said, I'm all for young 'uns learning and seeing the world, but seems like Henry should be in charge of who goes with him."

Henry shook his head in agreement. "I'll be gone two days. Teresa and Thad have chores to do."

"Thad, it seems like you and Teresa are wanting to do a lot of galavantin'. Henry's right: there's your chores. Anyone going anywhere on a work day has to agree to do his share of the weekday work on Sunday or Saturday afternoon. Them are the rules I'm making about time off. Get your chores done first. Henry's already put in two extra days, knowin' he'd be gone.

"I'm now adjourning this here first Meeting of the Clan. Thad, it's time to play your harmonica again. Hold on a minute until I get me drum."

Things certainly were changing.

The next morning we all went down to the Mullan Road with Henry while he waited for the stage to Rathdrum. We kissed him goodbye and sent him off in a flurry of good wishes.

Thad and I wished we were going – anywhere, just to be going.

Two days later in the evening Emmy had gone to bed, Thad was working on his lessons by lamplight, Mama was at the table darning socks and I was in my room about to get ready for bed when Lucky began to bark.

"Henry's home!" Emmy shouted and leaped out of bed.

The front door opened and a tired-looking Henry came in.

"We could have had Charlie and the cart meet you at the Mullan Road if we had known which stage you were coming in on," Mama said hugging Henry.

She began laying out supper for him as we all bombarded him with questions.

"Is Rathdrum like the Valley?" "Did you see the new school?" "Did you get lost?"

I wanted to say, "Did you get the job?"

But there was no need. Henry wasn't Henry and that meant the news wasn't good.

"Tell us all about it," Mama said.

"I'll be like Papa Willie when there's a story to tell," Henry said. "Let's go outside in the grove of trees where it's cool and watch the moon rise. I'll tell you all about it."

Mama and Papa Willie sat on the bench Henry had made and the rest of us lounged on the soft moonlit grass.

"First off, you didn't ask how I made out. You most likely knew I didn't get the job for this year – but maybe next."

"That's better than nothing," Papa Willie said.

"How come?" Thad asked.

"Tell us about Idaho," Emmy said putting three buttercups in Henry's hand.

"Idaho is wild country," Henry said and Papa Willie shook his head in agreement. "The roads are nothing but trails. I could have made better time by train. All the same I would like to have gone on to the town called Coeur d'Alene."

"Can we, some time?" Thad interrupted.

"Let Henry talk, Boy," Uncle Willie admonished.

"The school was new, barely finished and set in a grove of trees like this only larger. Lots of tamarack along with the cedar and fir. I could see five farms off in the distance but near enough so pupils could walk to and from school. The rest will come on horseback. There was a row of hitching posts off to one side of the school proper.

"The superintendent hadn't had but one other application for the job. It was from a lady. He wanted a man. That got my hopes up. He said there would be two mighty big boys in the class and doubted a lady could handle them. I was hopeful.

"But when I told him I had been studying by myself since we moved from New York, and hadn't yet finished my high school courses, he started questioning me more closely on what books I was studying and what I read. He said by law a teacher was supposed to be eighteen and have passed graduation examinations."

"See, Thad," I said. "We need to go to a real school."

"Listen to your brother," Papa Willie admonished again.

"I'm eighteen," Henry continued, "so that was all right. But listening to him, I knew he thought I needed more studying before I was ready to take the state tests.

"That's exactly what he told me. He said he would hire the lady temporarily, but hoped I would apply after I passed the state tests. Teresa is right. If there's a school being built around here, Thad and Teresa and Emmy should go."

"Couldn't you promise him that you would take the tests before school opened?" Mama asked.

"Seems as if the lady has already passed the state tests."

"Are you and Eloika still going to marry?" Emmy asked.

"I hope so, but I don't know when." Henry stretched out in the grass as though he were very, very tired or very, very sad.

Thad and I laid back too. I whispered to Thad, "Let's sleep out. The moon is so pretty tonight."

Henry continued, "There's another problem about me marrying Eloika. Her family is going to move off their farm down into the country near DeSmet. Many of the Coeur d'Alenes have already moved there to escape the encroachment of white settlers. Both she and I are too unsettled to think any more about marriage right now."

Henry sounded so sad.

"Let's all go to bed now," Mama said, "and let

Henry have some peace and quiet. He has a lot to think about."

"Thad and I are going to sleep out in the tepee tonight, Mama," I said.

"Me, too, Mama?" Emmy asked.

Mama nodded.

No one asked Henry anything else. We all knew how much he had counted on getting the job so he could marry Eloika. I was sad, too — to hear that Eloika was moving away and I wouldn't be able to have my Chinook lessons. I would miss Mama Anna and Keena and Eloika.

I caught hold of Papa Willie as he prepared to go into the house.

"What about exploring, Papa Willie? Thad and I want to explore down Trent way this week-end. We'll start Saturday afternoon with Luke and camp on the south side of the river Saturday night and come home across Spokane Bridge on Sunday."

"Can't spare Thad on Saturday afternoons until the garden's in," Papa said. "After you two and Eddie Chuck get the roots grubbed out, there will be rocks to clear, the ground to be broken, and rocks to clear again for a good seed bed. Eddie, Thad and I will do that while you help your mama. The rock hauling is man's work. You'll have to hold off exploring."

Settlers had to work hard to survive. Thad and I were well aware of that. But we never thought we would have to work this hard.

Our boss, Edward Chuck, BB was a hard task master. "Black Robes showed Eddie how work," he said.

"Pick up rocks. Pile for fences. Eight inches break soil. Pick up rocks."

"These rocks are breaking my back," Thad complained.

"Papa Willie say 'Do,'" Eddie Chuck answered severely.

I told Eddie about Thad's idea to water the garden with ditches from our stream. He helped Thad dig the ditches and showed him how to guide the water with a shovel.

When the water tumbled unobstructed in ditches between our freshly planted rows, Eddie said, "Good job!" imitating Papa Willie and smiling a somewhat toothless smile.

"Eddie Chuck," I said. "Could you show Thad and me how to build a canoe?"

"No time till work done. What for canoe?"

"If we had a canoe, we could cross the river any

time wherever we wanted and wouldn't have to pay toll."

"River dangerous. Where you want go?"

"We don't want to have to go all the way to Spokane Falls or Spokane Bridge to get across."

Eddie shrugged. He and Thad went on with the garden work.

I was glad I wasn't a boy. "When all that's done, will we be able to go exploring with Luke on a Saturday afternoon and Sunday and camp out for the night?" I asked Papa Willie.

"Sounds like how I would have wanted to explore at your age," Papa Willie answered.

Now and then Luke came by expecting that finally Thad's Saturday afternoon work was finished and we could go to Trent. When I told him it would be a while before that could happen, he took me aside and said,

"Tress, I have a load of cordwood to deliver just beyond Trent today. I've been hearing that something's going on there. Why don't you get Charlie and the cart and follow me? We can both park at the railroad bridge and walk across the river on the tracks. After we find out what's what, I'll go on and deliver my wood and you can go back home."

"I don't know about walking on the railroad bridge. Mama and Papa wouldn't let me if they knew. And what about Thad? It wouldn't be fair to go without him. He wants to know about the warehouse as much as I do."

"We won't tell Thad. He doesn't have to know. Nobody does. We'll tell your ma you're going to visit my ma at my house for the afternoon."

52

CHAPTER 7

A Narrow Escape

Mama said she didn't need me for the afternoon and gave me some bulbs and a jar of currant jelly to take to Luke's ma.

When we got to Trent, Luke tied his team to a pine tree and I parked Charlie and the cart on a trail nearby. I stayed in the cart, looking at the Spokane River and then at the railroad bridge. I wished I had told Mama and Papa Willie where I was going.

"Luke, let's not," I said. "I don't want to walk across that bridge."

"C'mon, Tress. There's nothing to it. Your Mama and Papa Willie will never know. You're almost fifteen. When are you going to start thinking for yourself?"

"I am thinking for myself. I'd rather swim across the river than walk across that railroad bridge. What if the train comes along?"

"I checked the schedule. It won't."

"Well, what if it does?"

"Then we would jump off into the river. We can both swim."

"The water is cold."

"It isn't far to shore. If we sit here arguing for two hours, the train will be coming."

Luke pulled me out of the cart and down the trail. I tried to go back.

"Are you going or not?" he said. "If we're going to cross, we've got to do it now. If I'm gone too long delivering this wood, my pa and ma will want to know where I've been. I'm going across. C'mon."

"I'm going to see how cold the water is," I said. I ran away from him down to the edge of the river. He followed me.

"Nobody's going to fall in the water," he said as I leaned over and put my hand in. "I've walked across that railroad bridge before and never came near falling in the water. Nothing to it. You're wasting time. You said you wanted to know what's being built on the other side of the river. This is the only way you'll find out."

Luke walked to the beginning of the bridge incline. "Are you coming with me or not?"

"The water's not very warm, Luke. I'm scared."

"I'm going across. "

"I'll wait here and watch for trains."

"Do what you want. I'm going."

He looked up and down the track. I looked, too. Nothing coming. He climbed onto the tracks.

I called after him, "If you're doing this for me, Luke, don't do it. I can wait to find out what's being built until we figure out a better way to cross the river."

"I can see the roof from here through the trees," he called, now on the track above the river. "Axtel was right. It isn't a warehouse. It's a house."

"BE CAREFUL and hurry."

I watched, clenching my hands.

"Hurry," I called again. *Oh, Luke, why are you doing this? Don't you know that you mean more than the warehouse to me? I couldn't go on living if you drowned.*

Soon he was across and jumped off the train track. He looked back and waved at me and disappeared into the trees.

Relieved that he had made it across, I sat down on a rock at the edge of the river and waited for him to return. My eyes didn't leave the spot where he had disappeared.

How I wished we hadn't come. Even if a warehouse were being built at Trent, Thad and I couldn't work there. How could we get there every day? We couldn't walk that far in winter weather, and Mama and Papa needed Charlie and the cart on the farm.

Of course, there was the new team Aunt May and Uncle Ray were supposed to buy for us with our Christmas money from Grandma in New York. When we got that team, we could ride those horses everywhere. But Mama would probably think even that would be too dangerous with all the miners on the road.

Suddenly I stood up. What was that clicking sound? I looked down the track in both directions. Luke had just come out of the trees and climbed onto the bridgework again.

It couldn't be the train at this hour, but the whirring, clicking was getting louder.

The sound was exactly like metal wheels on a track.

Then it came into view – a railroad hand car speeding toward the bridge. It was manned by two workers who rode the rails at regular intervals watching for trouble spots.

"Luke, Luke," I yelled. "Go back. Look!"

"Stop! Stop!" I yelled at the hand car workers.

No one heard me. I yelled again and again and waved my hands madly, toward the approaching hand car with no success.

"Go back. Go back. A hand car! A hand car!" I yelled to Luke.

He heard me.

"I can make it!" He started to run from tie to tie.

"Don't run! You'll fall in the river. Go back!"

My warning was too late.

He stumbled.

I closed my eyes.

A splash!

The squeal of the hand car wheels on the rails.

The voices of the two railroad workers.

I didn't dare look. I heard rocks tumbling down to the river.

I opened my eyes. Luke was in the fast moving water clinging to a floating log. The men were at the river's edge.

"Let go," one worker bawled to Luke. "The current is pulling you toward a rock. Let go. Catch the rock. Then catch this."

He held out a stout tree branch.

Partly swimming, Luke let go of the log and let the current carry him to the rock. With his back hard against the rock and paddling with one hand to keep afloat, he grabbed at the branch until he caught it.

"Hold on," I screamed. "Hold on."

With both men tugging and hauling and Luke hanging on to the branch and kicking his feet, he soon floundered onto the stony beach.

He lay there a minute or two and then struggled to his feet.

"Are you all right? You're a good swimmer," the tallest workman said, "but a fool hardy boy. It's not easy to keep your head above water with all them clothes on. What were you doin' on that bridge anyway?"

The other man broke in. "It's a dang good thing we're not the law. You'd be on your way to the lockup. Walking that railroad bridge is against the law.

Get yourself home and take care of them scratches."

Luke's pantleg was torn and his leg scratched and bleeding.

He didn't seem to notice it. He thanked the men, said he was sorry he delayed them and assured them he wouldn't walk the bridge again.

"I just wanted to see if I could do it," he said.

That wasn't exactly the truth, but I didn't correct him. I was too happy that he was safe.

The men grumbled some more about being delayed, went back to their hand car and disappeared in the trees on the other side of the river.

I said to Luke as I sat on a rock beside him watching him pour water out of his shoes, "You could have hit your head on that log or landed on a rock."

"Well, I didn't."

"Let's not tell Mama and Papa Willie. They wouldn't ever let me come with you again. Did you see Axtel or his family?"

"His house wasn't as near the road as it looks from the mountain. I couldn't get down his path. Parked wagons blocked the way. It would have taken too long to go around them. There was some kind of a meeting going on in a pasture. A lot of shouting. I'd like to come back tomorrow and find out what that was all about."

"Don't, Luke," I begged. "It's too dangerous."

"Dangerous, afraid. Are you almost fifteen or aren't you? When are you going to grow up, Teresa?" Luke limped back to his wagon, untied his horses, got in his loaded wagon and I heard him drive away. I didn't see him go because of tears in my eyes. He didn't even say good-bye. I had never felt so lonely.

I should not have come.

I slowly trudged back to Charlie and the cart and drove hard all the way home, hoping, hoping that no one asked me anything about where I had been.

Thad met me at the top of the hill.

"Where have you been, Tress? I've been looking for you. The garden is ready for planting. Papa Willie and Mama are going to inspect it. I may be able to get next Saturday off and we can go on that camping trip with Luke."

"Luke is mad at me," I said. "He probably won't want to go."

I swore Thad to secrecy and told him what I had done. As much as I always hated to let him see me cry, I couldn't help it.

CHAPTER 8

The Two Faces of Luke

PAPA WILLIE, MAMA and Eddie Chuck were in the garden when Thad and I got there.

"How did you find the Aarons, Teresa? Is Liza feeling well?" Mama asked methodically. All her attention was on Thad's new watering system.

"Liza is well enough," I said.

"Henry an' me finished the new addition this afternoon," Papa Willie said. "Your mama will be moving out of your room soon. You and Emmy will have the girls' room all to yourself."

"Thank you, Papa Willie," I said, so glad I wasn't asked any more questions about my afternoon.

Papa Willie watched the water run into the ditches from our stream. "Good job, Eddie Chuck," he said.

"Eddie didn't do it all," I said. "It was Thad's idea."

"I meant the 'Good job' for all three of you," Papa said. "Henry will be working on the new barn now that the new room is done. Teresa, you and Thad had best start helping Henry. As soon as it's finished, the old lean-to will be your new home, Eddie, if you want it."

Eddie nodded, "Good job!" His eyes flashed with the warmth of a *thank you* as they had when Marshal Warren told him he was a free man. Now that

61

the black paint was off Eddie's face, he looked like any other farm worker. I had gotten used to his Small Pox scars and no longer noticed them.

Thad and I liked working with Eddie. He told us about Indian history and legends — of Chief Circling Raven who ruled the Coeur d'Alenes for one hundred years from 1660 to 1760. Eddie promised to show us how to weave baskets when we were snowed in next winter.

"Do Tress and I get this Saturday afternoon and Sunday off, Mama?" Thad asked. "We want to get started exploring down by the railroad bridge."

"Your papa always said, 'All work and no play makes Jack a dull boy.' Time now for a little play. What do you say, William?"

"They did a good job on that garden."

"I worry about them walking across that railroad bridge. Seems like they could explore around here."

"We won't be walking across it, Mama," Thad said. "Luke is taking his wagon and a load of cordwood to Spokane Falls. We'll cross the river at the Post Street Bridge in town, go straight to the marshal's office and leave off the wood. Then we'll drive along the south side of the river to the railroad bridge and camp there Saturday night. Sunday we'll do our exploring and come home, crossing the river at Spokane Bridge. We'll have to be gone Saturday afternoon AND Sunday."

"Sounds like you've planned it all out, but crossing at Spokane Bridge with a wagon will cost $4, you know."

Thad looked sheepish. "That's the one thing I haven't planned out – where to get the $4."

The $4 toll at Spokane Bridge had always been a problem. Although we had gone to the Bridge regularly for provisions and the mail, none of us had ever driven across the bridge. The General Store and blacksmith were on our side of the river. Whenever we asked Mama if we could ride across the bridge "just once," her answer was always the same: "No need to cross. You can see the other side from here. We spend money only for necessities."

"About that four dollars," Papa Willie said. "You two know I'm all for young'uns getting out on their own. You're just about the age I was when I took me drum and went off fightin' in the Civil War. I've never been sorry. Thad, now that the addition is ready, I'm going to need help moving in. I ain't spent me last fifteen-dollar-Civil War pension check. You and Teresa help me with me moving and it will earn you exactly $4."

"Thanks, Papa Willie," Thad said. "Thanks. I didn't know how we would get that money. Tress and I will take Charlie and the cart up to your cabin and bring whatever you want down to the new addition whenever you're ready."

It was so good to have Thad including me in his plans. He, at least, was still my friend. Luke hadn't come near me since the day at the railroad bridge and I could hardly face Mama and Papa Willie: I still hadn't told them about that awful day.

"You'll have to ask Luke if we can go with him Saturday," I told Thad. "He'll say *no* if I ask him."

Why had I let Luke persuade me to go on that bridge-walking escapade with him?

Papa Willie continued to talk to us about his plans. "Won't be bringing none of the animals down from me cabin except Mabel me horse and me cow and chickens. Me buddies, Martin and O'Malley will be livin' in the cabin and will take care of me sick animals for a spell."

"Are you going to sell your homestead, Papa Willie?" Thad asked.

"Not yet. Not 'till Martin and O'Malley gets settled some place else. They've lived with me since our prospectin' days and don't take to me getting married."

"We could plant your land in cattle feed and let your buddies stay on in exchange for caring for the place, William," Mama said.

"Don't know yet how it's all going to work out here," Papa Willie said.

"Why, William, what does that mean?" Mama asked.

"Don't know yet if I'll have time to take care of me old place and this place too."

On Saturday I was happily surprised when Luke, his wagon loaded with wood to take to Spokane Falls, appeared on our back road soon after lunch. He acted as though nothing had happened between us.

"Tress, you and Thad sit on the driver's seat with me," he said. "We'll load Elliot Vandersims' map and our tent and camping gear under the seat."

I told Mama not to worry, that Luke was dependable and away we went, down the hill onto the Mullan Road toward Spokane Falls.

There was not a sign of a cloud in the sky. As usual when riding, Thad took out his harmonica and I began to sing "Sod Shanty on the Claim," a song Papa Willie had taught us during the winter. I sang as loud as I could, all three verses with the chorus between each verse:

"I am looking rather seedy while holding down my claim
And my vit'ls are not always served the best
And the mice play shyly round as I settle down to rest
In my little old sod shanty in the West.

"I rather like the novelty of living in this way
Tho' my bill of fare is always rather tame
I am happy as a clam on the land of Uncle Sam
In my little old sod shanty on the claim.

"When I left my eastern home, a bachelor so gay
To try to win my way to wealth and fame
Didn't think I would resort to burning twisted hay
In my little old sod shanty in the west.

[Chorus]
"The roof is made of sod and straw
The window has no glass
I hear the hungry coyote
As he sneaks up in the grass
Round my little old sod shanty on the claim."

An Indian woman galloped past us. Standing up behind her on the horse and holding onto her shoulders was an Indian boy about four. He waved to us plodding along with our loaded wagon and team.

"Sing good!" the woman called.

"Looks like they're practicing for the Fourth of July Pow Wow at Spokane Falls," Luke said.

"Eloika told us about that PowWow. I'm going to ask Papa Willie if I can go this year for my birthday," I said.

"Good idea," Thad agreed.

"Sing that song again so I can learn it," Luke said.

I sang not only that song again, but taught Luke other songs Papa had taught us. We sang lustily and happily all the way to Spokane Falls.

This was the old Luke, the Luke that was so different from the Luke I first met who hated Indians and the Luke who suggested that I lie to Mama and Papa Willie. How could the same person seem at times like two different people? Today's Luke was the Luke I always had a good time with.

Why was I thinking these thoughts about Luke? I wasn't perfect. I was the one who had lied to Mama.

When we arrived at the Falls, I was sorry the ride was over.

Thad and I got out of the wagon and walked along the shore line looking for arrowheads for Thad's rock collection. Luke told us where to wait for him while he delivered his wood. When he came to get us, his wagon was empty.

"Sold my whole load to the marshal," he said, obviously proud of himself. "Let's head for the trail on the south side of the river."

"What about the map?" I asked. "Shouldn't we look for Mr. Vandersims?"

"I asked about him at the marshal's office. The marshal knew him but said he also knew that he would be on the road today showing property."

"Did you ask him about the warehouse?"

"The only new building he knows of along the river at Trent is a home being built by a settler from Minnesota."

"That would be the Stebbins house," I exclaimed. "What shall we do with the map?"

"Keep it until Mr. Vandersims comes for it."

We piled into the wagon and soon were riding on the south side trail with the sun at our backs.

"We won't make Trent before dark," Luke said. "Best to camp for the night somewhere along the river."

"How about where the four trails come together? Where we first met Papa Willie? The place called The Four Corners."

"A good place to water the horses and let them graze."

Luke agreed. "There will probably be other travelers stopping there for the night. We can ask them if they know of a warehouse being built near the railroad bridge."

At The Four Corners amidst other wagons and horses parked for the night, we found a grassy spot for our camp.

We put up our tent, swam in a shallow edge of the river, built a campfire and were sitting on the bank eating our beans and fried sow belly when a heavy wagon with a heavy load pulled up not far from us.

"That's a dray," Luke said. "Somebody must be moving."

On the side of the dray was printed FRED GATLEY'S STORAGE AND TRANSFER COMPANY.

"He might know what's been going on at Trent," Luke said. "Let's go talk to him."

CHAPTER 9

Wilhelmina Fredericka Gatley

IN A LOUD and commanding voice, the driver of the dray shouted, "Whoa."

As I watched *him* slide off the driver's seat, I couldn't believe my eyes. Where had that voice come from? The *he* was a rosy cheeked, raw-boned, jolly-looking *she*. Her brown hair had been pulled up under a wide-brimmed Stetson, uncontrolled wisps decorating her face here and there. Her red striped shirtwaist clung to her well developed body under bright yellow suspenders that held up an ankle-length deer hide skirt. The *she* looked capable, strong, and colorful.

She paid no attention to our surprise. She held her head high, breathed deeply and sighed with satisfaction. "That's hot coffee brewing that I smell or my name isn't Wilhelmina Fredericka Gatley."

Her round brown eyes sparkled as she breathed deeply again, looking with pleasure at our coffee pot and bubbling pan of sow belly and beans warming over our makeshift campfire.

She showed her approval by bringing forth from the abyss of her wagon a tin plate, cup and eating utensils. Without waiting to be invited, she poured

herself some coffee and spooned herself some beans.

Then she settled her generous self on the stump of a tree near us.

"Freddie Gatley," she said after draining her coffee cup and refilling it without hesitation. "If you're somewhat surprised to find Fred Gatley is a *she*, pay it no mind. Fred Gatley is my daddy and a fine man. I rode with him in the dray from the time I was weaned from my mama's milk. Now daddy's lumbago has laid him low, and I'm a-taking over his business and doin' every bit as good a job of it as he did — though it is best not to tell him I said so. Being on the road from sun-up to sun-down most days leaves me little free time for cooking, and I do appreciate home cooking. With you sharing your supper like this, I'll be able to get right to bed and be on the road by sun-up tomorrow morning without losing so much as a wink."

Freddie motioned toward the dray. "Have a fearsome load this time. Needs to be delivered by sun down tomorrow. No room for victuals and no time to fix them if I had them. I'm beholding to you for sharing yours."

She set her drinking tin on the ground and stretched out her hand. We all shook it, introduced ourselves and Thad said we were pleased to make her acquaintance. Although I can't say that I liked how Wilhelmina Fredericka Gatley helped herself to our supper without being invited, I liked her.

As she ate our beans, she talked:

"Daddy and Mama came to Spokane Falls from Missouri. Mama died soon after I was weaned off her milk. Daddy took it on himself to raise me. Took me everywhere him and his dray went."

She stopped eating and looked us over. "I know every twist and turn of this river. Fact is I call the Spokane River *friend.* I ride along and talk river talk and sing river songs. We're arm in arm, me and that river. My daddy says what I need is a good man, but to this day I haven't met up with one who compares to the river for companionship."

Luke cut in, "You heard of any building going on at the new settlement they call Trent?"

"There's building everywhere in the Valley. Soon there won't be a place free for a man to lay his head. There's a store, a depot and a saloon going strong at Trent."

"Mama says the Trent store is not much of a store. We shop mostly at the Bridge."

As Freddie started to answer, a smart looking rig, the horses galloping, dust flying, drove past on the main trail not far from where we were camped. The driver held the whip firmly and a passenger called out to Freddie and waved. The rig flew down the road before she could return the greeting.

"That's Cash-up Vandersim's outfit," Freddie said. "He's sure in a hurry to get where he's going. Most likely some meeting or other."

"Did you say Vandersims? Vandersims was the name of a man who upset his boat on our beach. Said his name was Elliot," Thad said.

"Cash-up or Elliot. No difference," Freddie said. "Cashup is what the settlers calls him. Lots of folks finds fault with Cash-up but I understand what he's about. Isn't easy to get money for your work from settlers. Cash-up, he has a rule and abides by it: says 'no deal unless you show me the cash up front.' That's why settlers calls him 'Cash-up'. Everybody knows Cash-up Vandersims. Smartest businessman in these parts. Miners, when they strike it rich, look up Cash-up to find them a spread. But settlers, hard put for cash, have no use for him. Some say he's slick. I say he's a right smart businessman. Cash-up and me, we've worked together time and time again. I've got a soft spot for the old goat. I ain't good at collecting debts an' he's the best. Every settler in this here Valley has owed me and my daddy money at one time or another. But, Cash-up? No siree. He tells 'em without batting an eyelash, 'Got to have the cash up front.'"

"He doesn't know how to handle a boat or the river, Freddie," Thad said.

"Never knowed Cash-up to spend much time on the river unless he's sizing up property for one of his business deals," Freddie said.

Thad told Freddie how we happened to have a map that belonged to the man *we* called Elliot Vandersims but *she* called Cash-up Vandersims.

"He didn't tell us his name was Cash-up."

"Lordy, no."

"Have you made many deliveries at Trent, Freddie?"

"You can just bet I have. On property where Indians pitched tepees last year. The railroad land for sale there has brought folks of all kinds from all over the country. Last month I delivered two railroad cars of household goods and four fiddles for some folks from Minnesota. I never saw so many fiddles in one place. I was thinking they might be folks wanting to entertain at the saloon."

"Or maybe they're wanting to start a school band," I suggested hopefully.

"Interested in a school, are you? Start your own. Folks are doing it all over this valley. In barns, any

old shack — just wherever there's an empty building. So many of my customers asked me how to get
money from the government to pay a teacher that
in my wagon I carry a page of writing about starting a public school. Its free for the asking."

"I'd like to have one," I said.

Freddie pulled a red bandanna from the pocket
of her skirt and wiped her mouth. She stood up.
"Glad there's a way I can repay you for the beans,"
she said. "I'll be getting you that sheet of paper
then I'm turning in for the night. My daddy taught
me 'Early to bed, early to rise, makes a man healthy,
wealthy and wise.' That saying goes for us of the
fairer sex, too." She chuckled a big, broad chuckle.

She continued. "If any of you young folks are ever
into town looking for work, my daddy is always
needing help. Call at Fred Gatley's Storage and
Transfer, near Front and Howard, near the Falls.
Tell daddy you fed Little Freddie one night on the
road. That'll set well with Daddy."

Freddie brought us the pamphlet and said good
night. We watched her drag a bedroll from the dray
and spread it out under the wagon. "Just in case it
rains," she called and disappeared.

"We'd best sleep under our wagon," Luke suggested.

We did; and as it turned out, we were glad we
did. The ground was wet in the morning. There had
been a shower during the night and we never felt a
drop. It was Freddie pulling out that wakened us.

"She's nervy," Luke said, "but you've got to give

her credit. She's doing a man's job and not whimpering about it."

The trail on the south side of the river was bumpy with dried-mud ruts and led through gentle rises of bunch grass. While the boys took turns driving, I read to them the pamphlet that Freddie had given me.

"It says, 'Settlers who are interested in the education of their children must decide where their school will be located. Then they must call a meeting to elect people called directors. The directors must make a list of the children who will attend the school and decide how much to pay a teacher and where the money will come from — from taxation or by voluntary contributions.'"

"Can you make sense of that, Tress?" Luke asked.

"Sort of," I said. "But there's more. After all that is settled, the heads of the interested families have to sign a petition saying they want to start the school. Probably something like Steve Liberty's petition about reservation boundaries. The petition has to be taken to the county superintendent."

"I'd like to do that," Thad said. "Id like to see a county superintendent. Remember, Papa Willie saw his County Superintendent when he went to school in the Blue Mountains?"

I gave the paper to Thad. He was engrossed in it as we neared the railroad bridge. I was sitting next to Luke. He reached over and squeezed my hand. "Don't let on that I've been here," he whispered.

"Do you two have secrets?" Thad asked.

"Sort of," Luke said looking at me in a way I liked.

Luke tied the horses to a tree near a path crossed by the trail we were on. It was obvious that on the north side the path led to the river.

We followed it on foot and at the river came upon a flat bottomed row boat bottom side up on the bank.

"Belongs to someone who lives near here," Luke said. "It is well used. If we want to find the owner, we'll need to go back and follow the path on the other side of the trail."

We returned to the horses and moved them to a grassy spot near the boat and near the water. Then we took Luke's advice and set out to explore the path on the south side of the trail.

CHAPTER 10
Problems

W E WALKED quickly. When we came to a pasture with wagon ruts and the grass trampled down, Luke whispered to me that we were on the right path. This was the place where he had come upon a meeting of some kind the day he walked across the railroad bridge.

We hurried on and soon reached the end of the path and a partially completed two-story cabin.

In the yard, four red-haired boys played Annie Annie Over. Instead of a ball, they threw the stuffed half-foot of an old sock over the cabin roof.

I immediately recognized the tallest boy as Axtel Stebbins.

Under a shady maple tree, on a large roughly hewn picnic-like table lay four fiddles of various sizes. In a rocking chair nearby, a neatly groomed auburn-haired woman in a colorful long, flowered calico dress sat knitting. At the edge of the yard a middle-aged man in work clothes with a sun shade pulled over shaggy blond hair sawed a board supported by two saw horses. Seeing us, he laid down the saw and walked toward us.

I nudged Thad. "It's Axtel's father! I saw him at the Bridge."

The man said, "I am Oliver Stebbins." He motioned toward the woman knitting, "That's my wife, Nella."

He looked hard at me. "You're the young lady whose groceries my son, Axtel, spilled at the Bridge."

I nodded and both Axtel, who had joined us, and I laughed.

"We meet again," he said. "Father, this is Teresa Wickstrom and her twin brother, Thaddeus. This is their friend, Luke. We all met on the mountain the day I drew the map for you."

Oh, yes," Oliver said. "I remember, you told me."

The other three boys stopped their game and joined us.

Oliver Stebbins said, "These also are my boys — Abraham, Asa, and Avery. Axtel is the oldest. He is fifteen. Abraham is the youngest. He is eight."

At last, I thought, somebody for Emmy to play with. "I have a sister seven years old," I said.

"Sit down," Oliver Stebbins said, motioning to the benches around the picnic table and a bench near the door. "The fiddles belong to the boys. In Minnesota they played at picnics and dances as The Fiddlers Four. Nella and I hope they can play in the parade at the Fourth of July PowWow at Spokane Falls."

From out the open screen door came a pretty, smiling girl. Her hair, like her mother's, was auburn, but had golden glints.

"And this is Sarah, my only daughter. She started high school back home," Oliver said proudly. "You live near here?"

"Up on Northwood Prairie," Thad said, "It would be near if it weren't so hard to get across the river at high water.

"We have to go all the way to Spokane Falls and

come around. We don't get on this side of the river often. Luke had some cordwood to sell in Spokane. We came along with him."

"We're exploring," I added. "We saw your roof, Mr. Stebbins, from the look-out on our mountain. We hoped it was the roof of a warehouse; but I see, as Axtel told us, it is your home."

"I'm afraid it won't be our home for long," Oliver Stebbins said. I remembered how disturbed Axtel was on the mountain when we talked about his house.

Nella Stebbins laid her knitting in her lap. "We came West from Minnesota to be near Oliver's father," she said. "Ten years ago he established a homestead farther on up the road. We brought the family here last month to be near him. He's getting on in years and his health is failing. Oliver and I wanted the children to grow up knowing their only surviving grandparent."

Oliver grinned sheepishly. "There was another reason why we came West," he said. "We had a 320-acre farm in Minnesota and I'm just not a farmer. The farm wasn't doing well. Father wrote us of the warehouse to be built here at Trent and plenty of railroad land available cheap. I saw my chance to change jobs and be near father. I was able to buy this land and got the promise of a job at the warehouse when it is built."

"We want to get a job at the warehouse, too," I said.

"Trouble is, it looks like the warehouse won't be built because of a recording mistake at the courthouse," Nella said.

"When this land was sold to us, the sale was not recorded," Oliver explained. "The developers of the proposed warehouse unknowingly bought the same property from a Mr. Vandersims."

"Seems like that could be straightened out," Luke said. "Give the warehouse people their money back and sell them another piece of land."

"This is the property they need — close to the railroad and the river. They want me to sell it to them."

"But you have your cabin on it. What will you do?"

"We may let the warehouse buy this land and go back to Minnesota," Oliver said, "because that isn't my only problem."

I was beginning to understand why Axtel looked worried when we talked about his home before.

Oliver Stebbins lifted his well worn sun shade and rubbed his forehead. "It's this second problem that has me buffaloed."

"They don't want to hear our troubles, Oliver," Nella said.

"I do," I said. "Maybe Mama and Papa Willie can help. Here on Northwood Prairie we all help each other."

Thad told the Stebbins how the settlers had helped us move our cabin. Luke told them how Keena had helped his mother get well when she had pneumonia. Oliver responded:

"When Nella and I first talked about moving West to be near father, I made a promise to her that seems to be impossible to keep. I promised her that the boys would be enrolled in a public school in time for the September term. Now we find that the nearest public school is in Spokane Falls. To go to school there would mean daily trips on horseback."

Nella interrupted, "I won't have the boys making

that trip in all kinds of weather and meeting up with Indians and who knows what else along the way."

"The Indians won't bother," I said. "We have Indian friends."

"We're a family of stubborn people. Nella insists that I keep my promise. She plans to return to Minnesota if the boys are not enrolled in a public school by September. How can I enroll them in a school when there is none near? None of us want to go back to Minnesota. I've even thought of starting a school of my own; but because our home is here, it would have to be on this property. Then the warehouse wouldn't have the land they need. No warehouse would mean no job for me."

"I can't have the boys missing out on their schooling," Nella Stebbins insisted. She rocked and knitted with vigor.

"Mother never lets us miss a day of school. I think we should start our own school on another piece of land even if it wouldn't be ready by September," Axtel said.

I thought of the pamphlet Freddie Gatley had given us.

"We have a paper in our wagon that tells how to organize a school. It might help," I said.

"The woman who transported our belongings from the railroad station gave us a pamphlet about that," Oliver said. "We could do it, but not before September. We would have to find a site for both a new cabin and the school, enroll students, see about getting text books, hire a teacher — all in addition to actually building a home and the school.

Pretty Sarah interrupted: "I can study on my own. I'm willing to stay here with Father this winter if he lets the warehouse have this land and builds a new home and the school on some other property. Mother and the boys could go home to Minnesota for the winter and come back when everything is ready. I want to stay here. I like to draw. There is so much beautiful scenery here to draw. But Father does not want to stay without the boys. He feels that he could not get along without the whole family here with him."

Oliver Stebbins nodded. "My family and I are one. If Nella and the boys go back to Minnesota, I go with them."

"You will leave your cabin and your father?" I asked.

"I want to stay so badly," pretty Sarah said.

"So do we," Axtel said.

"The boys like the open country. I believe a school will come, even within the year, especially if the warehouse comes. Settlers arrive every week. A year of home schooling shouldn't hurt Sarah or the boys. I can't convince Nella of that."

"To make up for the weeks of school the boys lost when we left Minnesota, I have been encouraging regular lessons," Nella said. "But there are too many distractions. The boys have trouble putting their minds on books with all of this land so new to them. Our home schooling has not been successful."

"It isn't fair to have to have lessons in the summer," Abraham said.

Again Mr. Stebbins took off his cap and rubbed his forehead.

"We have school every evening," I said. "We do our lessons faithfully enough to please Mama and Papa Willie. I'll bet your boys will, too, after a while, Mrs. Stebbins. They just haven't been here long enough to get used to their new home. Mama didn't start us studying the first summer we were here. At first there's too much to see and do to study."

Thad said, "We want a school as badly as you folks do. I want to learn more about rocks and minerals in a real school so I can go on to college. Our real Papa used to say, 'Two heads are better than one.' Maybe if we all work together, Mr. Stebbins, we can make a school happen before September. I'll bet Papa Willie will help. If we Wickstroms help, do you think you could get a school organized by September and get your property troubles straightened out?"

"I'd be willing to try," he said.

We talked for a long time telling the Stebbins all about coming from New York and about getting Uncle Willie for a new papa. We talked until Luke reminded us it was time to leave.

Nella stopped knitting. "Oliver, I'll give you till the end of July to decide what to do about the boys' school. I'd like to stay as much as the rest of you, but more important is the boys' schooling. Some day they will be the wage earners of their families."

"Mother, no more lessons this summer. Please, Mother?" Abraham begged.

"We'll continue with home lessons until we see what comes of all this talk," Nella said picking up her knitting again.

Luke moved toward the path. "I need to get going."

"Wait just one more minute." Sarah said.

She went into the house and came out shortly with glasses for everyone and a pitcher of lemonade. "Something to wet your whistle before you start off," she said.

After the cool drink, Sarah went back into the house again. This time she came out with a crayon sketch of the Spokane River just as we had seen it — with the upside down rowboat on shore and the sun glistening on the water.

"This is why I want to stay here," she said. "There is so much beauty here. I promised Father and Mother that I will continue drawing even though there is no art school nearby, if only they will stay."

"I learn on my own," Luke said proudly. "I'm learning my pa's trade. I don't need no schoolhouse to learn."

Did I imagine it or did I see Luke and the pretty girl exchange smiles?

"But if you get a school going," Luke said looking straight at Sarah, "I might ask my pa if I can come — although my pa's not much for schooling. He thinks learning the carpenter trade is all the schooling I need."

Luke, showing an interest in schooling! Just what I always hoped he would do. Or was it Sarah he was interested in? Maybe I did the wrong thing offering to help the Stebbins start a school so they could stay. Luke was *my* friend. I didn't want him smiling at Sarah Stebbins.

CHAPTER 11

Crossing the River

"HAVE TO BE going," Luke said reluctantly.

"Mr. Stebbins, when we came, we saw a rowboat near the river. Could we use that boat to get across?"

"The river's pretty swift. What about Luke's team and wagon. You couldn't put them in the rowboat."

"A team and wagon can cross at the ford at high water if there's a fearless driver and the team is used to wading," Axtel said.

"My horses have waded now and then," Luke said. "But I've never driven them across the river when it was this swollen."

"With Luke's help, I could take the team across," Sarah replied.

"She's a fearless driver all right," Oliver Stebbins said proudly. "Want to let her try?"

"We were planning on crossing at Spokane Bridge, but that costs toll money. If we cross here free, we can save Papa Willie's four dollars for another time," Thad answered.

"I'm sure Luke and I can get the team across," Sarah said. "Axtel, you help Teresa and Thad in the rowboat."

Two oars stood by the door. Sarah and Luke each picked up one. Luke said to Sarah, "I'll carry that," and they started down the path side by side. Axtel and Thad walked together and I came trailing behind them.

Axtel and Thad talked noisely about the possibility of starting a school. I tried to hear what Luke and Sarah were saying. Their voices were too low but I was sure they weren't talking about the school.

As we came in sight of the rowboat, Luke, in answer to a question Axtel called to him, said, "I don't rightly believe my pa will let me go to school, but I sure would like to see a school nearby for your brothers and Thad and Tress and Emmy; and I hope you folks don't have to go back to Minnesota." He looked at Sarah as he said that. My heart sank.

I chimed in quickly, "Papa Willie won't let Thad and me have many Saturday afternoons and Sundays off to help with the school."

"I think he will," Thad said. "He's all for education. This is a good time of the year to help, Tress, before the garden needs cultivating and we get going full tilt on the barn."

Axtel, Thad and I turned the rowboat over and untied it. Sarah untied the horses and she and Luke climbed into the wagon.

"What's this under the seat?" Sarah asked. "It might get wet."

"Our tent and provisions and the map," Luke said. "Let's put them in the boat."

One by one, he handed Thad, Axtel and me everything that was stored under the driver's seat.

"The wagon seems light now," Sarah said. "Too

bad it isn't heavier. It will sway when we get in the current."

"I'll come with you," I said. "That will make it some heavier. Thad and Axtel can bring the rowboat across."

"Stay with Thad and Axtel, Tress," Luke said. "At high water like this, it's dangerous for wagons to cross, even with the best of drivers. Ride where it's safe."

"Sarah's not riding where it's safe," I said.

"She's different," Luke answered.

"Giddap," Sarah said, taking the reins as if trying to prove his words.

The horses snorted and balked at the water's edge. Sarah cracked the whip in the air and Luke urged them into the flood.

In no time they were swimming and the river water was almost higher than the wagon wheels.

Axtel pushed the rowboat off. "Hurry, jump in," he said. "They might need our help."

Thad and I scrambled for a seat as Axtel handed Thad an oar. "Tress, get up in the stern," he ordered. He and Thad, sitting next to each other, began to row, following as near the wagon as possible. It rocked perilously.

"Tress, get up here with Thad. Take my oar," Axtel said slipping out of his boots and shirt. He jumped into the river swimming as close to the wagon as he safely could.

"Keep rowing," he called to me and Thad.

The wagon rolled and tumbled. Luke and Sarah slid from side to side on the driver's seat, constantly shifting their weight, trying to keep the wagon on an even keel. Sarah held the reins, urging the horses ever forward through the onslaught of the current.

When the horses stumbled up the opposite bank jerking the wagon behind them, Luke looked at Sarah with admiration.

"You don't look like a horsewoman," he said. "but it took some first-rate knowledge of the river and of horses to do what you just done."

"It isn't easy to keep a wagon right side up at high water," Axtel said.

"We had horses in Minnesota." Sarah flushed with pride. "I like the river. Axtel and I swim across often. I knew I could take the team across."

We transferred our belongings back to Luke's wagon from the rowboat.

"Will your father sell your property if you go back to Minnesota?" Luke asked.

"Father's idea is to hold onto the property until there is a school nearby unless it is absolutely necessary to sell it to the warehouse company."

"I hope you can stay, Sarah," Luke said again. And again my heart sank.

"Get aboard," Luke said to me and Thad. "I gotta be goin'."

From the wagon, Luke called to Sarah and Axtel who were getting ready to recross the river in the rowboat, "Let me know how I can help with the school."

"How about building some desks?" she called joking.

"I just might do that," Luke answered. He watched and waited until the rowboat crossed safely, then called a last goodbye and started the team on the homeward leg of our journey.

Sarah called to him, "You helped with the crossing, too, Luke. Come again, all of you."

"We will," Luke answered.

That Sarah Stebbins is a flirt, I thought. I decided then and there that I didn't like her. But I knew Luke did.

All the way home, Thad talked about the school. He and Luke said they were going to try to find students and look around for a teacher.

I didn't talk. I was no longer anxious to help with the school. I was losing Luke to Sarah Stebbins, I knew it. Luke, the only friend I had my own age.

I wished there were some way we Wickstroms could have our own school and Luke could go to it if he was so interested in school. I wished I hadn't ever asked him to bring us across the river to the Stebbins' homestead.

Thad's voice cut into my thoughts. "Tress, what would you think of asking Papa Willie if Mr. Stebbins could use his cabin for a school?"

"Why Mr. Stebbins? Why don't we start a school there ourselves and forget about the Stebbins? Let them solve their own problems," I said.

"We've already told them we would help. Uncle Willie's cabin would make a great school," Thad insisted. "I'm going to ask Papa Willie if he has made any plans for his cabin. If he hasn't, I'll ask about having school there."

LOVE ACCORDING TO TERESA

"You'll have to do the asking. I'm not having anything to do with the Stebbins' school. But I'll help if we start our own."

"What difference does it make whose school it is? We'll all help and we'll all go," Thad said with feeling.

When we arrived where our trail took off from the Mullan Road, Luke said, "What's that sign on the tree?"

"It says MEASLES! Why would it say that?"

"Because somebody around here has the measles and is quarantined," Luke said. "And I'm not going any farther. When I'm delivering my wood and see that sign, I stay away. I'd best not take you the rest of the way home. I don't want to go anywhere near the measles. You can walk up your hill, can't you?"

"I remember those big black-on-yellow signs in New York," I said. "My friend, Wanda, had measles. She wasn't allowed at school for two weeks. Who could have it? Nobody lives up this hill but us."

I stood still, frozen with fear. "NOBODY LIVES UP THIS HILL BUT US," I repeated.

CHAPTER 12

Measles!

"NO ONE IN OUR family has the measles," Thad puzzled.

"You mean nobody in your family had it when you left," Luke said. "Say, didn't you say Henry hadn't been feeling well since he came back from Rathdrum?"

"That was because the superintendent said he would have to graduate from high school before he could teach there. He moped around because he was disappointed."

"Maybe not," Luke said. "That measles sign is right under the sign you made, Thad, that says WICKSTROMS and the one Willie made that says WHITEHOUSE. Somebody in your house MUST have the measles."

"What should we do about it?" Thad asked.

"I know what I'm going to do," Luke said. "I'm going to get home. You two can walk up your hill and find out what's what. Maybe it's just a joke, but I don't think so. The sign is yellow on black same as the signs saying CHICKEN POX that I've seen in Spokane Falls. No one is allowed in or out of those houses for two weeks, sometimes three."

"Not allowed in or out for two weeks? That would be terrible. We couldn't get a school started," said Thad. "What shall we do?"

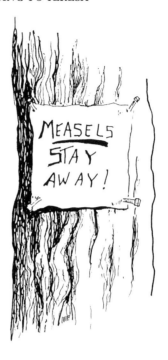

"I know what I'm going to do," Luke said again. "I'm staying away till you come and tell me the coast is clear. I'll get my water at the ford in the river. No telling when the quarantine will be lifted. Could be longer than two weeks if more than one has the measles. Your tent and camping things will be too heavy to carry up the hill. I'll keep them for you until the two weeks is up."

"Couldn't you take us part way, Luke?" I asked.

"I suppose part way, but not right up to the barn. They say them measles can fly around."

When we were within sight of our cabin, Thad and I got out. Luke put our camping gear on the ground without so much as a Good-bye-I'll-see-you-soon and turned the horses around.

He looked sober as he drove off toward his house. I felt depressed. The idea of being quarantined was bad enough, but not knowing when I would see him again was the worst. I watched him go as though I were taking leave of someone I would never see again.

"What shall we do, Thad?" I rubbed the back of my hand across my eyes so Thad wouldn't see tears.

"Come on, we've got to find out who's got measles. Don't start crying."

We trudged the rest of the way up the hill.

At the edge of our clearing, Eddie Chuck met us. "Where tent?" Eddie asked without even greeting us.

"Back there a ways. Does somebody have the measles?"

Eddie nodded. "Henry. Doctor from Fort Coeur d'Alene checking houses. People in Rathdrum sick. Henry sick."

"Where are Papa Willie and Mama and Emmy?"

"Mama and Emmy not come out of house. Papa Willie at his house."

"You mean Mama and Emmy are quarantined, but Papa Willie is living at his house?" Thad asked.

Eddie nodded. "Me not quarantined. Me live in barn. Papa Willie say he come soon with groceries to leave on front porch. He say you put up your tent. Look! Papa Willie come now."

Sure enough, up the hill came Mabel pulling Papa Willie in his cart. We rushed to meet him.

He confirmed all Eddie Chuck had told us. There was a measles epidemic in Rathdrum spreading to other areas fast. The doctor from Fort Coeur d'Alene was making the rounds, telling the settlers how to care for the sick. He posted quarantine signs wherever there was sickness.

Henry, apparently, had contracted the disease while at Rathdrum interviewing for the teaching job there. Emmy and Mama had been with Henry when he became feverish. Because we had not lived at home the last two days, we would not be quarantined if we stayed out of the house.

"I want to help Mama with Henry," I said. "I don't want Henry to die." Tears streamed down my face.

"The doctor from the fort told your mama what to do," Papa Willie said. "He said measles is harder on grown-ups than young 'uns and Henry is pretty sick. But he'll most likely get well. His fever is going down. You and Thad have a choice. If you don't go into the house, you can live in the tent and go about your business and not be quarantined. If you go into the house, you will be quarantined, too."

"What about you, Papa Willie?"

"Wasn't here the last couple of days when Henry broke out. Been up to me cabin getting things ready for you young'uns to help me move. I'll be able to bring your ma provisions and check on things long as I don't go inside. Her and Emmy and Henry is the ones that's quarantined. I'll be staying at me cabin till it's over."

"Poor Mama and Emmy," I said. "They'll get it from Henry, won't they?"

"Your ma won't. She's had the measles, same kind as Henry has, so chances are she won't get it again. Can't say about Emmy. She's likely to come down just about the time Henry's up and around. That's how measles works."

"Thad and I have had measles," I said quickly. "We don't have to worry."

"There's red measles and black measles and reg'lar measles and some other kinds. You'd best stay away. Henry likely has a different kind than you had, getting it from Rathdrum like he did."

Thad and I looked helplessly at Eddie and Papa Willie. None of us spoke,

Finally Thad said, "I'm for pitching the tent, Tress. You and I can live in it and cook over the campfire."

"I'll go to the Bridge tomorrow and get us provisions. We still have Papa Willie's four dollars he gave us for toll. I'll tell Mama Anna. Maybe Keena knows some Indian medicine that will keep you and me from getting sick. But I don't think so. I've heard Eloika say the Indians never had measles until the white man came. Maybe Mama Anna won't want me to come for my Chinook lesson."

"I hear measles is hard on Indians and they don't know nothin' about the sickness," Papa Willie said.

As tired as we were, Thad and I set up the tent.

News of our quarantine traveled fast. The next day when I went to the Bridge for provisions no one wanted to get near me. Only Mr. Cowley at the store was friendly. However, even he met me at the hitching post.

"I'll fill your order and bring it out to you," he said. "I ain't afraid of measles for myself. Had it twice already. But you'd best stay away from my customers."

There were two good things and one very bad thing about the measles quarantine. The very, very bad thing was that Luke no longer came for water. The good things were that Papa Willie said he would stay in the tent with us after we helped him bring his belongings from his cabin, and that Eddie Chuck, because he lived in the barn and not in the house where Henry was, was not quarantined. With him, Thad and I worked every day on the new barn. We wanted to visit settlers with children in the evenings and tell them about the new school, but we weren't welcome. So we put all thoughts of helping with the new school out of our minds.

Eddie became mysterious. He wouldn't let us near the lean-to barn that had become his home. At night in our tent, sometimes we heard what sounded like scraping.

One day Thad said to Eddie, "Are you making something, Eddie?"

"Fixing up new tepee," Eddie said.

"Want us to help?" I asked.

Eddie shook his head. "Big surprise," he said. "You not see till finished."

When we asked Uncle Willie if we could visit the Stebbins while the quarantine sign was on our tree, he said, "Eddie is your boss till the quarantine is lifted and your ma can have a say."

Thad told Eddie about wanting to help Mr. Stebbins start a new school at Trent. I told him I wanted to start a school, too, but not at Trent.

Thad said, "Tress, let's not worry yet about where the school will be. Let's work together to get enough pupils and decide that later."

That sounded good to me, so Thad asked Eddie if he could spare us part of Sunday to go to the Stebbins.

"If work done," he said mimicking Papa Willie. "But maybe Stebbins not want you around."

"If we get a school started, would you want to go, Eddie?" I asked.

"When?"

"Not now. The school isn't built yet," I said.

"When work done," Eddie answered.

Thad and I sighed. We knew Mama and Papa Willie always agreed on decisions about us. Now Eddie Chuck had joined their ranks. "When work done" seemed to be the answer to everything, no matter whom we asked. We knew Eddie wouldn't consider "work done" until the new barn was finished.

Thad and I didn't mind living in the tent at all. Ever since coming to Northwood Prairie, on hot nights we had often slept in the tent. The thing we didn't like about the arrangement was being separated from the rest of the family.

We usually spent our evenings studying our

school books, but they were in the house. So we filled our evenings helping Papa Willie move his belongings from his cabin to our property.

We couldn't put his things in the house, so we stacked his bed and bureau and odds and ends under a tarpaulin until the quarantine was lifted. We set up his table and chairs outside our tent near the firepit and had our meals on it.

All in all, the quarantine, except for worrying about Henry, was an adventure. Regularly Mama and Emmy came out on the porch and waved to us and we talked at a distance, shouting to each other.

We learned a lot about measles from Liza, Luke's mother, who visited us in the tent now and then. I asked her about Luke. She said he was working hard cutting and selling wood, that he didn't want to come for water because he had had only three-day measles and was susceptible to Henry's black measles, the most serious kind.

"Where is he getting water?" I asked.

"At the ford near Trent."

That meant he was seeing Sarah, my worst fear.

Liza told Mama she should not leave us notes on the porch because one of the ways the disease was spread was by handling things the sick person had touched.

Our dog, Lucky, came and went freely, but we didn't pet him. We were so afraid of the contagious disease.

We learned that one of the greatest dangers of measles was the damage light could do to the eyes. Mother kept the curtains drawn. It was spooky looking at our cabin with the windows covered. It seemed like a deserted house.

We were always happy when Emmy and Lucky came out to play or when someone went to the outhouse and there was life around.

One day Mama and Emmy were working in the flowers. I started to run toward them. Then I remembered.

Thad spent whatever spare time he had with his rock collection. Luckily, he kept it in the barn and was able to get to it.

We lived in the tent for almost a month. Just when Henry was well enough to wave to us from the porch, Emmy came down with measles. Mama called to us not to worry, that Emmy was not as sick as Henry had been.

The new garden, watered with Thad's irrigation ditches, grew well and we began weeding and cultivating it. With Eddie Chuck's help we finished the new barn but he still didn't allow us into his lean-to barn-home. That puzzled us more and more, especially since we were sure, from the noises we heard, that he was building something. We frequently thought we smelled burning pitch.

There was no hope of doing anything more about a school until the measles quarantine was lifted. I saw Axtel at the Bridge. Even he kept his distance and said it would be best not to visit until things were back to normal at our house.

No one wanted us around even though Thad and I weren't quarantined.

I didn't see Luke during that long, long time. But I thought about him often. In my thoughts he was always with Sarah. And she was always even prettier than she had been when we met her. I hated those thoughts.

CHAPTER 13

A Special Day

IT WAS BARELY sunrise. Something had awakened me. Papa Willie! What was he doing up so early? He went outside, was gone for about half an hour, then came back. He didn't go back to bed.

He tiptoed noisely to the bedroll where Thad lay sound asleep. He shook Thad until he stirred. He whispered something in his ear.

Thad got up and dressed quickly. They both went out. What was going on? Had Emmy taken a turn for the worst?

I jumped into my clothes and headed for the house.

Suddenly the hills resounded with Papa Willie's drum roll and Thad's harmonica.

A meeting of the clan? This early?

The door to our cabin flew open and Mama, Henry and Emmy in their nightwear, sleepy and bewildered, stood on the porch exclaiming almost in unison, "What's wrong?" "What happened?" "Why are you up so early?"

Above the drum roll Papa Willie shouted, "The quarantine is lifted! We're free! We're free!"

Such a lot of kissing and hugging there was.

We gathered around Papa Willie.

"The doctor from Fort Coeur d'Alene came by

early this morning and took the sign off the tree. This calls for a meeting of the clan. Addy, get the skillet. Henry, if you feel good enough, build the fire in the pit. We'll all have breakfast together outside at my table. Teresa and Thad, set the table."

There was another drum roll. Then Papa Willie said, "Who knows what the date is?"

"We looked at each other. We had forgotten about dates. Every day had been much the same since the quarantine.

Then I remembered. But it couldn't be!

"Thad, it's Fourth of July! Our birthday!"

Papa Willie laughed. "Never heard of young'uns forgetting their birthday. Thad, run to the barn and get the flag."

"Fifteen! We're fifteen, Thad."

"I'll have to make a cake," Mama said.

"The sign is gone. Ain't that present enough?" Papa Willie asked.

Just then, Eddie Chuck came out of his lean-to barn-house. "Look down hill," he called.

We ran to the edge of our clearing.

TWO teams trudged up our road. Lucky ran headlong down the hill barking at the second team.

"It's Uncle Ray and Aunt May," Thad yelled turning a cartwheel. "But why are they each driving a team?"

"Happ-y birth-day," Uncle Ray called.

"I know why there are two teams," I shrieked. "One team is ours. Aunt May is driving a team for us, isn't she, Mama? The team Grandma sent us Christmas money for?"

We forgot about the breakfast cooking and ran down the hill to meet Uncle Ray and Aunt May.

"Good thing your birthday is a legal holiday. Would have had a hard time getting a day off," Uncle Ray said. "Mill is busier than I've ever seen it. Folks moving in faster than the drays can haul their belongings to their homestead."

"Eddie, take that flapjack off the griddle. It will burn up," Mama called.

"Is this really our team, Uncle Ray?" Thad asked.

"Just look at that wagon. Painted green, my favorite color," I said. "And WICKSTROM on one side and WHITEHOUSE on the other in red paint. What are the horses names?"

"I want to name them," Emmy said. "I named Lucky. I want to name these horses. I want one to be named Happy and the other Birthday."

"Those are silly names," Thad said.

"I like Happy," Mama said, "I don't know about Birthday."

"Sounds good enough for now," Papa Willie said, "until we get to know 'em. Mighty pretty pair of matched bays."

"How about Happy and Merry?" Emmy asked. "Grandma gave us the money for our Merry Christmas."

"I like both of those names," Mama said. "What do you say, William?"

"Happy and Merry it will be until somebody thinks of better names.""

As time went by, the horses answered well to those names. And no one ever thought of better names.

"Thad!" I shrieked. "If we learn to ride Happy and Merry, we can go to Mr. Stebbins' school if he gets it going."

"Let's go to the Stebbins' this weekend now that the quarantine is lifted."

"If work is done," Eddie Chuck said. Papa Willie and Mama laughed and nodded in agreement.

We helped Uncle Ray and Aunt May tether all four horses in the grass by our spring. They joined us at the pit for flapjacks.

"You, too, Eddie Chuck," Papa Willie said. "No work today. Put down your hoe. We're celebratin'. No more measles sign, Thad and Teresa are fifteen years old and we have a work team. Yes sir, we're celebrating."

Eddie Chuck nodded. "Me know about birthday," he said. "Have surprise. All come."

Papa motioned to Thad to play his harmonica. He played a song we all knew, "The Bear Went Over the Mountain." We had taught it to Eddie while we worked in the garden.

To the rat-a-tat-tat of Papa Willie's drum and the rhythm of Thad's harmonica, we marched behind Eddie to the lean-to barn, singing

"The bear went over the mountain
The bear went over the mountain
The bear went over the mountain
To see what he could see.

And all he saw when he got there
And all he saw when he got there

And all he saw when he got there
Was just the other side."

At the barn door, Eddie stopped. "Look," he said pointing to a rough sign over the door. It read, *Eddie Chuck, BB.* "Me Barn Boss," he said proudly.

We clapped and Emmy called, "Hooray for Eddie." We turned to leave.

"Wait. This not the surprise." He went into the barn and came out dragging . . . A CANOE! A beautiful hand-made canoe.

Light and graceful. Neat patches of white, red and gray paper-birch sewed together and glued on the skeleton with pitch from the forest.

"It is beautiful, Eddie Chuck," I said. I touched it softly as though I were feeling velvet.

Eddie grinned happily. "Good canoe," he said. "Will cross river at high water. Papa Willie say, 'Keep for birthday party.'"

"Papa," I said, "you knew about this and never told us!"

Papa Willie grinned.

"Now we can cross the river without going to the Falls or the Bridge," Thad said as though he could not believe his good fortune.

"Go to Spokane Falls today," Eddie Chuck said.

"Why, Eddie?" Mama asked. "What do you mean?"

"Big horse races always at Spokane Falls on Fourth July. Everybody go from everywhere."

"The Fourth of July celebration at the Falls. Of course," Mama said. "How could we forget. Liza said there will be races of all kinds and the Indians will be in their full regalia. We missed it last year. What a nice way to celebrate Teresa's and Thad's birthday. Let's all go, William . . . But there won't be time to bake a cake."

"I'd rather go to the races than have a cake, Mama."

"Me, too," I agreed hastily.

"The races usually last more than one day. How about staying in town over night with us?" Aunt May invited.

We all chorused, "Yes, yes!"

"Think the garden can spare us for two days?" Papa Willie asked.

"Yes! Yes!" we all shouted again, including Uncle Ray and Aunt May and Eddie Chuck.

"Then we'd best get our breakfast out of the way and change our duds and be on our way," Papa Willie said. "We'll have to finish the meeting of the clan another day."

"Teresa and Thad will ride in the new wagon with me," Uncle Ray said. "I'll teach them to handle Happy and Merry."

"When back, I teach handle new canoe," Eddie Chuck said. "Canoe for crossing river to go to school."

"Are you going to school if we go, Eddie?" I asked.

"When work done," he said.

We hurried through breakfast although Mama insisted on taking time to put birthday candles on a big flapjack while everybody sang "Happy Birthday" to Thad and me.

While we got into our visiting clothes and packed a carpet bag for overnight, Uncle Ray and Aunt May looked at Thad's rock collection. Emmy picked an armful of wild flowers – her present for Thad and me. Aunt May put them in an empty can with water so they wouldn't wilt while we were gone.

Our real Papa, in bad times, often had kept our courage up by reminding us, 'After the storm, comes the sun.''

The sun had certainly come out on Northwood Prairie. We had a new team and wagon and were going to the famous horse races at Spokane Falls. We had a new canoe and no more quarantine. We were one family again – and Thad and I were FIFTEEN.

I had another secret reason for being happy: Luke would be able to come to our spring for water again . . . if he wanted to . . .

CHAPTER 14

Fourth of July at Spokane Falls, 1887

W HEN ALL HANDS were dressed "in their best bib and tucker" (as Papa Willie put it), Mama, Papa Willie, and Emmy climbed into Uncle Ray's and Aunt May's wagon with Henry driving. Thad and I sat high beside Uncle Ray and Aunt May in our very own new green wagon. "Pay attention to how these horses handle," Uncle Ray said.

Eddie Chuck, long black braids flowing over his shoulders, followed on his crippled horse, Tikut. Tikut was an Indian word meaning elder.

"Her an old mare," Eddie Chuck answered when questioned about the name.

Henry led our little parade down the hill to the Mullan Road where we stopped to allow a party of Indians in full ceremonial dress pass by. Among them was an Indian we didn't know by name, who must have been one of the subchiefs, we decided. He was astride a huge stallion. Two shiny black braids hung on his shoulders from a magnificent eagle feather headpiece. He wore a beaded buckskin vest and trousers, moccasins with tiny silver bells and wrist bands decorated with porcupine quills and tiny shells.

We fell in behind the Indians, but they soon out-distanced us. We drove slowly, enjoying the early morning fresh air.

A settler family from the hills in a farm wagon, three miners from Idaho riding their mules, and a group of soldiers from Fort Coeur d'Alene all passed us.

Eddie Chuck was right – everybody was going to the Fourth of July celebration at Spokane Falls.

At Trent I asked Uncle Ray to drive Happy and Merry to the river's edge, so I could show Mama and Papa Willie where the Stebbins lived across the river and where we hoped we would be able to visit again soon.

"The property seems too near the railroad track for a school," Papa Willie remarked. "Good spot for a warehouse."

As we neared Spokane Falls, all kinds of con-veyances driven by all manner of people clogged the road. From the Post Street Bridge on into town, horses, people and their wagons jockied for space.

The traffic pulled over to the side of the road as a procession led by Civil War veterans came into view. It was followed by rigs decorated in red, white and blue carrying the city fathers and Frank Dallam, the founder and editor of the *Review*. He wore his usual long tails and pants in his boots.

"A parade! A parade!" Emmy cried, rocking the wagon as she jumped up and down and clapped her hands.

Down the street came horse-pulled fire wagons from the two competing fire companies in town. They clanged their bells as their horses plodded down wide, but jammed, Front Avenue. The men on the truck lettered Fire Company No.1 wore blue shirts, white belts, and white helmets while the men on truck No.2 wore dark blue shirts trimmed in red with black helmets.

"There's the fire chief, E.B. Hyde," Papa Willie said. "Good man! Look at them fiddlers up the street coming in front of the Salvation Army band. They sure can fiddle."

"It's Axtel. Axtel, Axtel! " I called and waved.

"Abraham! Avery! Asa!" Thad yelled. "They're playing 'Turkey in the Straw.'" We yelled and waved again but they didn't hear us. They didn't look to the right or left.

The town Salvation Army band played "Onward Christian Soldiers" and as it passed us, "Rock of Ages." We had sung those two songs at our Sunday School in New York City. When onlookers sang along with the band, we did, too.

"See them cowboys across the way?" Papa Willie asked. He pointed out riders in broad-brimmed Stetson hats. "They're from down Walla Walla way."

Eddie Chuck had watched the Fourth of July doin's the year before from a hiding place among a clump of trees on the Riverside Avenue rim. He was our source of information. He led Tikut, first to Uncle Ray's wagon and then to ours, telling us there would be all kinds of events from Indian free-for-alls to horse and buggy races.

"Race not just for white men. Indians in races, too. Many races. Horses running, trotting, pistol shooting. Studded gold belt for shooting winner."

111

He explained to us as best he could that the most popular event of the day was the horse race that would start soon in the town center at Papa Glover's general store and corral near the river on Howard Street.

"Race stay on bluff above south Spokane River bank, west to Hangman Creek. There make curve south. Follow Hangman Creek bluff. Fourth Avenue race winds, turns east, fast back to starting line at Glover's.

"If room left," Eddie Chuck continued, "stand near Fourth Avenue. See end good there. Put horses and wagons in livery stable near there."

So we headed for Fourth Avenue. Uncle Willie led us through the motley crowd that partied in the streets.

Luckily there was room for our wagons at the stable.

As we walked to the viewing spot on Fourth Avenue that Eddie suggested, I noticed the decorated store fronts and the displays in harness shops along the route — all kinds of fancy harnesses and buggy whips with silver plaited handles.

"Must be a lot of money in this town if they expect to sell those," Papa Willie said. "Look there."

Elegantly dressed gentlemen and ladies waited for the start of the race from gay-painted, spindle-wheeled buggies harnessed to high-spirited horses in a roped off area along the way.

"Them are most likely members of the Spokane Gentlemen's Riding Club. I've heard tell that riding is the top sport of the rich in this here town these days," Uncle Willie said.

"I wouldn't trade Happy and Merry and our shiny new wagon for any of those rigs," I said. "I wish I'd see Luke. I want to show him our new wagon and tell him we won't have to ask to borrow his any more."

"Is that the only reason?" Thad teased.

"Yes," I answered curtly.

On Fourth Avenue we joined the crowd of onlookers. I scanned the crowd to see if I could see anyone I knew – especially the Stebbins . . . and Luke.

"Look, Mama," I said. "See that small, slick-haired man in the high black felt hat talking to those men in Prince Albert coats? His name is Cash-up Vandersims. He's the man who lost his map in our river."

"You're right, Tress," Thad said. "I wish we had thought to bring his map along. I'm going over there and tell him we found it."

Thad elbowed his way through the noisy crowd. He returned shortly not only with Cash-up in tow, but also with Freddie, the draylady who had eaten our beans and drunk our coffee. He introduced them to Mama and Papa and Aunt May and Uncle Ray and Eddie Chuck.

I told her I saw the fiddlers marching in front of the Salvation Army band.

"Good to know they weren't headed for some saloon," she said.

"Bound to be a good race today," Cash-up said. "May I inquire how you folks are betting?"

"We're not betting," Mama said. "We're just watching. We came to celebrate the twins' birthday."

"Any favorites?" Papa Willie asked.

"Now, William," Mama said.

"The town's riding club members are taking bets on a sleek looking stallion entered by a cattleman from Walla Walla. Fine piece of horse flesh. The soldiers have their money on a sleepy-eyed, long-legged gelding that they've named Soldier. You'll know him. He has a USA brand on his rump. Looking at him, you'd think he couldn't walk, let alone run. But I never sell the soldiers short."

"You mean you're for Soldier?" Papa Willie asked skeptically.

"Yes, I'm going with Soldier," Cash-up said. He winked at Papa Willie. "Inside information."

"I've got a Silver Eagle burning a hole in my pocket."

"You know I don't like gambling, William," Mama said.

"Money put in Cash-up's hands ain't no gamble, Missus," Freddie said. "There's nobody knows better what to do with a Silver Eagle than my friend Cash-up Vandersims."

"That cinches it," Papa Willie said. "Place my bet, Vandersims." He handed Cash-up his silver dollar.

"No hard feelings if Soldier doesn't come through?" Cash-up asked.

"No hard feelings," Papa Willie assured him.

In the twinkling of an eye, Cash-up and Freddie disappeared in the crowd.

"Oh, William, I wish you hadn't, " Mama sighed just as a shot followed by a shout such as I've never heard before or since shattered the air.

"They're off! They're off!" the crowd yelled.

Until the five racing horses actually came into view, we followed the race by the shouts of the onlookers.

The cattlemen's horse was ahead as the galloping steeds led off and rounded the first corner. The cattlemen were still ahead as their horse came into view, raising the dust in front of us.

"Guess Freddie and Vandersims didn't know what they were talking about," Papa Willie said. "There goes my Silver Eagle."

"William, serves you right. You know I don't cotton to gambling," Mama said.

The cheering and shouting became deafening. Added to that noise and the pounding of the charging hoofs was the revelry of a group of cavalry officers down the rim not far away enjoying a barbecue and beer bust.

Suddenly amidst the din, a pistol shot!

Simultaneously, Soldier spurted ahead of the pack as though he had been shot from a canon.

Papa Willie grabbed Mama. "Did you hear that? Did you see that?"

"I heard a shot, William," Mama said. "Those revelers down the rim, wasn't it?"

"Did you see Soldier move? Look at him go!"

Although the horses were out of earshot, Papa Willie jumped up and down and cheered, "That's it, Soldier. Bring my Eagle back home."

The pistol shot had been lost amidst the uncontrolled cheers of approval and disapproval. Anyone not standing where we were, could not have heard it.

Soldier never stopped galloping until he crossed the finish line at Glover's stable.

"The Winn-ah — Soldier from Fort Coeur d'Alene, Idaho Terr-i-tory."

Jostling through the crowd toward us came the beaming Freddie with Cash-up in tow.

Cash-up pressed two Silver Eagles into Papa Willie's hand.

"Doubled your money, Friend," said Cash-up with satisfaction.

"Nothing like knowing horse flesh," Papa Willie winked at Cash-up.

"Why, what are you saying, William?" Mama asked.

"He just means, Mrs. Whitehouse, that before you bet, you should know what or who you're betting on." Cash-up winked at Papa Willie again.

"What's all the winking about?" Mama demanded. "William, if that race wasn't fair and square, you're to return that extra Silver Eagle to its owner."

"Mama, if there had been anything illegal, the racing committee wouldn't have declared Soldier the winner," Henry said.

"Looked like Soldier had a good trainer. He was trained to sprint in the final stretch," Thad said.

"Exactly," Cash-up said. "Come on, Freddie. Let's situate ourselves strategically for the next race. Much obliged to you folks for safe-keeping my map. I'll be around for it."

Cash-up took a gold watch from his vest pocket, checked the time, and tipped his high black hat. Freddie waved good-bye. They were swallowed up in the crowd.

We watched other races that day and Mama made sure Papa Willie bet no more.

"You doubled your money. Be satisfied, William," she said.

Later that evening at the Harvestor house, Aunt May fixed us a supper of elk steak, boiled potatoes, cabbage, home-made bread, and canned peaches. Candles to celebrate our birthday again, found a make-shift home — on top of the loaf of bread before it was cut.

While Aunt May and Mama "cleaned up the kitchen," Uncle Ray took the rest of us for a walk to the Indian village by the river.

We talked about the day's races and the exciting finish to the horse race. "Soldier was a real sprinter," Thad said. "I'd like to own a horse like that."

Papa Willie mused, "In the Civil War there was many a horse as was turned away from service becuz it was gun shy. With all the shoutin' and confusion, like as not the judges never heard that pistol shot."

CHAPTER 15

A School or a Warehouse?

IMMEDIATELY AFTER breakfast, we said good-bye to Aunt May and Uncle Ray and piled into our splendid new wagon.

"We'll change drivers every four miles or so," Uncle Willie said. "That will give all four of you, even Emmy, a turn. High time she learned to handle a team. I'll drive the end stretch and take us right into the barn. I'm a-saying the driver can make the decisions about when to stop for a rest."

Thad, of course, had to be first.

"Papa Willie," he said, "could we go home on the south side of the river? I want to stop at the Stebbins and show them our new team and wagon and see if the plans for the school are coming along or if they are going back to Minnesota."

"The south road might be a nice ride for a change," Papa Willie said. "Looks like a scorcher of a day. The breeze is coming off the river from the north. That route will be coolest, but it will be longer. We'll have to go all the way to the Bridge to cross the river. My winnin's will help pay the toll at Spokane Bridge." He grinned at Mama.

Mama ignored Papa Willie's grin. "I'd like to meet Mrs. Stebbins."

"Hooray," Thad yelled. "It's settled. We finally get

to cross the river at Spokane Bridge. I want to drop the toll in Mr. Cowley's can."

"Could we take a swim at Sarah's ford and cool off?" I asked.

"Nobody has swimming suits along. Yes, Thad, you can pay the toll," Mama answered.

By the time we reached the Four Corners, we were tired, dusty and hot. I was driving, so I halted the wagon. We all got out, stretched and splashed river water on our faces to cool off.

I stopped for another rest where the Stebbins' trails took off from the road we were on.

"The trail to the left leads to the river and Sarah's ford where the Stebbins keep their boat," I explained to Mama and Papa. "It is near the railroad bridge. The one to the right leads to their house. There's quite a piece to walk to their house. Everybody coming?"

"I am," Emmy said. She hopped down off the wagon and started down the path. She had acted more grown up and self-sufficient since Papa Willie told her she could learn to handle the team.

The others followed Emmy, but Thad soon hurried in front. As we neared the Stebbins' home, he stopped and turned around.

"Be quiet!" he whispered.

The air was too hot for even birds to be chattering; yet we heard voices.

We stood still and listened. The voices came from around a bend in the path. Someone was either making a speech or reading something aloud to a group. The determined voice said:

". . . It's your choice. Do you want a school or a warehouse? You have been supporting Mr. Stebbins' school. That means he will not sell his property to my client for the warehouse. Just remember: a school means taxes. The warehouse means jobs and jobs mean more people. More people mean your land will become more valuable. It's your choice."

"The warehouse. The warehouse," someone shouted. There was another shout . . . and the clapping of hands.

"That speaker sounded like Cash-up Vandersims," I whispered to Thad.

"Be quiet. C'mon. Let's see what's going on."

As we rounded the bend, several horses without riders, others harnessed to wagons, and a team harnessed to a buggy contentedly grazed under shade trees in a small grassy pasturelike clearing.

Beyond, sitting on nail kegs, tree stumps, logs or lounging on the grass was a group of folks, obviously settlers.

Standing in front of the group was, just as I thought, Cash-up Vandersims. The same man we had seen only yesterday. In spite of the heat, he still wore his high crowned black felt hat, was in his shirt sleeves, red sleeve garters visible, his Prince Albert coat neatly folded on a stump nearby.

Near the stump stood Mr. Stebbins in work clothes like all the others.

"Next meeting will be in two weeks. Mr. Stebbins has promised to make up his mind by then. Same time, same place," Cash-up said, dismissing the group.

The group, all men, walked toward the pasture area, talking among themselves. They claimed their horses and wagons and rode away down the path we had come.

Cash-up Vandersims nodded in surprise as he passed us, then climbed into his black buggy with the sunshade down.

Mr. Stebbins waited until the last horse left before he approached us.

"Howdy," Papa Willie said. "You must be Stebbins. I'm Whitehouse and this is my good wife. She wants to welcome Mrs. Stebbins to the Valley. I hear you know my young'uns, Thad and Teresa. We're on our way home from the doin's at Spokane Falls. This here is Emmy and Henry. Since Emmy saw your boys marching in the parade, she wants me to get her a fiddle. Sorry if we poked our noses into some kind of a meeting just now."

"Let's all go to the house and have a glass of iced tea. On the way I'll let you folks in on what's going on here."

Mr. Stebbins pulled a red bandanna from his pocket and wiped his forehead. "Almost too hot to breathe. The house is at the end of this trail. We heard about your measles quarantine. Glad to see you all up and around, taking a turn for the better."

He wiped his sweaty forehead again and talked as we walked.

"What about the school, Mr. Stebbins?" I asked.

"The boys and I made good progress with it. I had a plan for the schoolhouse all laid out on that half of my property fronting the river near the railroad bridge. The boys and I approached neighboring settlers with the school idea and they were all for it. I had promises of volunteers to work on the building and money subscribed to pay a teacher. We were ready to approach the county superintendent."

"Good!" I said.

"But it seems like all that work was for nothing."

"How so?"

"The man who called the meeting you stumbled onto was Mr. Vandersims. He's the developer who sold my land by mistake to the warehouse company.

"Well, this fellow Vandersims sees I am not going to sell my land to the warehouse company and sees himself losing land buyers if that warehouse doesn't get built. So he talks the company into making me an offer I can't afford to refuse. In exchange for my property, I will get a new piece of property for my house and school in addition to a better paying job at the warehouse than the one they promised me. It would seem my problems are solved until you remember my promise to Nella. She agrees that the offer is generous but there still is the problem of this year's schooling for the boys. She will not stay unless the boys have a school this year. If I start over on new property, it will take me months to get my home and the school built. Nella will not wait. She plans to take the boys back to Minnesota. I must make my decision in two weeks or the warehouse company will look elsewhere for land.

"To make matters worse, Vandersims has gotten the settlers excited about the warehouse coming to Trent. He is promising jobs for all who wants them.

"He called that meeting to convince me and the others that a warehouse is more important to the community than a school house. A good share of the folks who promised money and help with the school are pulling out. They say their boys will learn the warehouse work without the expense of going to a school."

In the yard, the Stebbins' boys sat on benches at the picnic table shelling peas and cleaning potatoes. Nella, as when I first saw her, sat under the apple tree, knitting.

She smiled a welcome as we approached.

"How did the meeting go, Oliver?" she asked.

He shook his head slowly.

"Sarah," he called into the house. "We have guests. How about rustling up some iced tea for us?" He turned to his wife. "The company that mistakenly bought this land for the warehouse has spent a lot of money on plans and advertising back east. They need to know what I am going to do.

"Did you hear the applause when Vandersims finished his speech? The settlers want me to sell my property to the warehouse company. But there is no way I can build another house and a school all before September."

"The boys and I will go back to Minnesota for another year, Oliver," Nella said.

"We don't want to go back, Mother," the children chorused.

"Sarah will stay here with Father. We will come back next spring to a new house and school." Nella said firmly.

"I want to stay with Sarah and Father," Axtel said.

The screen door opened and Sarah came out with a pitcher of iced tea and glasses on a tray.

Following behind with a tray of cookies was . . . Luke.

If Mr. Stebbins said anything more at that moment, I didn't hear it.

Luke said hello to us, as casually as if we were strangers and he was meeting us for the first time.

My worst fear had been realized: while we were quarantined and he had been getting his water at Sarah's Ford, he had been getting better acquainted with Sarah.

"Father, I don't think the settlers are ready for the school," Sarah said. "Luke heard talk at the Bridge about your plans for a territorial school . . ."

Luke interrupted, "They're saying schools mean more taxes for the settlers. My pa agrees. He says there's plenty of homesteaders have barely enough money to buy food for their families. He don't want me to get no ideas about starting back to school. He says he can't spare me or the money."

"I know what they're saying," Mr. Stebbins said wearily. "Of course, I think they're wrong. Nothing is as important as adequate schooling for the younger generation. There are parents who are still with me. It's the miners and bachelors that are against me. That group owns a big chunk of the taxable property in Spokane County. They're not about to be taxed to educate young ones who have no claims on them. Cash-up is tied up tight with them. I say what with the county growing the way it is, there'll be need for a schoolhouse before the year is out."

Papa Willie lighted his corn cob pipe. "Almost too hot for me pipe," he said. "But me pipe helps me think and some of what you said deserves being thought about, Stebbins."

"If there's to be no school here, getting my boys back to Minnesota in time for the opening of the school year there is important to me," Nella said, her knitting needles clicking vigorously.

Luke was sitting next to Sarah with his arm around her waist. That was all I could think about.

CHAPTER 16

Love According to Eloika

As WE LEFT, I called to Luke and asked when he would be coming for water again.

He said, "I don't know." and did not explain.

I was miserably lonely. I felt exactly as I had when I said goodbye to my friends in New York before we came west.

As we drove into the yard, the momentary flush of excitement I had experienced because of finally crossing the river at Spokane Bridge faded.

Luke will never again come to our spring for water.

Lucky barked joyfully and jumped on me as he always did after I had been gone for a while. He licked my face. Tears that I had held back through the trip home cascaded down my cheeks.

"You've been lonesome here alone, haven't you, Boy? You were lonesome while I was gone, weren't you, Lucky? I'm back now. I love you, Lucky. I love you, Boy."

I hugged Lucky and buried my face in his coarse coat. It felt good to be close to something I loved. Luke was gone.

While I washed and Thad dried the supper dishes, he said, "We're fifteen now, Tress. Feels good, doesn't it? I'm going to ask Papa if I can cross into Idaho some weekend. I'd like to see what Fort Coeur d'Alene is like."

Luke didn't know that Thad and I had had a birthday. He didn't know that crossing the bridge at Spokane Bridge hadn't been fun for me because he wasn't along. He didn't know that the most fun for me at the races would have been seeing him. He hadn't been at the races. He had been at the Stebbins with Sarah.

Thad continued talking as he hung up the pans, even though I didn't answer. "Mr. Stebbins won't be able to get a school going by September. We might as well forget that."

I didn't answer.

"Don't you care that Mr. Stebbins won't have his school, Tress?"

"Thad, to tell you the truth, tonight I don't care whether he ever has a school or not. I just don't feel like talking. I wish Luke had been at the races."

"Forget Luke. I've been thinking, Tress. Maybe Mr. Stebbins could exchange his property for a piece of land with an old barn on it. That would do for a temporary school."

"Thad," I said emphatically, "Be quiet. I don't want to talk."

"Luke isn't everything. Aren't you glad we're fifteen? That we might be able to go to Coeur d'Alene by ourselves?"

"Didn't you see how Luke put his hand over Sarah's as she poured the iced tea? How he followed her with his eyes? Didn't you see how close to her he sat while we were talking?"

"What's wrong with that? I've seen Luke sit next to you in the wagon often."

"He hardly talked to me."

"Forget him. He's ruining our fifteenth birthday. You look like you've lost your last friend."

"I have. He likes Sarah."

"Tress, you're being ridiculous. If you're jealous of Sarah, there's no reason. Luke's a friendly fellow. He likes everybody. He wants to make the Stebbins feel at home on the prairie. He wants them to stay in the Valley because Mr. Stebbins is letting him log firewood off his property. He told me so."

"And because he likes Sarah," I said.

Thad shrugged. "I don't know about that." He threw the dish cloth down on the table and pulled his science book down off the shelf.

I put the rest of the dishes in the cupboard and hung the dish cloth to dry.

"Mama, I'm going for a walk," I said.

"Teresa, hadn't you best take someone with you? It will soon be dark."

"No, Mama, I want to go alone. I'll take Lucky. C'mon, Boy."

"Teresa, what is wrong with you?"

"Nothing, Mama. I don't want to talk. I want to be alone."

"Let her be," Papa Willie said to Mama.

I went outside and began to run with Lucky at my heels. As was our habit, we headed around to the back path that led through the forest toward the Aaron house where Luke lived.

The hot late afternoon sun hung low in the sky and burned red through the trees.

Lucky ran ahead, coming back now and then to nip at my heels as though to pull me where he wanted me to go. Blinded by the sun, and not caring where I ran, I followed him.

"Not so fast, Lucky," I said. I slowed to a fast walk.

I suddenly realized where we were going.

I stopped. "Not tonight, Lucky. If Luke is home, he doesn't want to see me. It's time to go back."

I turned around and trudged slowly back the way we had come. As always, Lucky understood and trotted at my side.

When we came to the clearing of old pines and firs that I called The Cathedral, I decided to rest. I found my favorite big old pine and sank down and leaned against the thick trunk. Evening breezes blew through the clearing. Lucky curled up beside me. I felt the warmth of his body against mine. I stroked his head.

He nestled closer. "I love you, Lucky," I said and wished I were saying it to Luke.

Hoofbeats brought me out of my reverie.

Lucky stirred. Then he stood up looking anxiously about.

"Do you hear something, Boy?"

I stood up. "Hoofbeats, Lucky. Let's see who it is."

We hurried out of the clearing.

I was relieved to see Eloika on her pinto but wondered what she was doing here.

130

She pulled up beside us. "Teresa, I'm so glad I found you. I went to your house first. Your mother told me you usually take this path."

"Is something wrong on the reservation?"

"Tress, I must talk to you." She dismounted.

"Come this way." I led her and her pinto into the peace and quiet of The Cathedral.

When we settled in the shady, cool hide-out, I asked again, "Is something wrong on the reservation, Eloika?"

"No, nothing like that. I want to talk to you about Henry."

"He talks about you all the time."

"That is why I want to talk to you, Tress. You know that he and I want to get married. He told me he needs me and can't live without me. But, Tress, Mama Anna and Keena and my people must move to DeSmet. It is my people's will that I go with them."

"Oh, no. How will we get along without you and Mama Anna and Keena, Eloika? I won't be able to have any more Chinook lessons. Everyone depends on Keena when they are sick. Oh, Eloika, your folks must not go."

"We must go, Tress. All our people must. We live in the path of the white man. The Black Robes have advised us to move to the south where our properties are protected by reservation boundary lines. It is sad, but we must go."

"Have you told Henry?"

"He knows that our people are leaving."

"Will you marry him before you go?"

"He will not marry me until he can provide a home for me."

"I don't know what to tell you, Eloika. It seems to me that you and Henry – not even your family – should be the ones to decide about your lives."

"I must abide by the decision of my family."

"Eloika, tell Henry that your family says you have to go and that you don't want to. He will be sad but he will go on living. Maybe he will change his mind and marry you now."

"If only he would. I worry about him saying he cannot live without me."

"Before our real papa died, he once said to us, 'Life has a way of filling up vacant spaces if we are willing to do the shovelling.' I haven't forgotten that.. Neither will Henry."

"But I don't want him to forget me."

"When Papa died, we worried about how we would get along without him. Now we have Papa Willie. But we remember our real papa too."

In spite of talking so bravely, just thinking about our real papa and how much I would miss Eloika and her family, made my eyes fill with tears.

She put her arm around me. "Henry will not be the only one with empty spaces to fill," she said. "But, Tress, I do worry about him. I want to have made his life richer, not emptier. Mama Anna told me, 'If you can not go on living when one of life's arrows is taken away, you have not adequately filled your quiver.'"

I tried to comfort her. "Henry has many interests. I know he has many arrows in his quiver."

"I am the one who will have to remember Mama Anna's words," Eloika said.

I put my arm around her.

"I have always asked myself so many questions about marrying Henry. We are so different, Tress. Would Henry like my people?"

"All of us already love your people. It is getting dark, Eloika. Mama, will be worried about me. I must go home."

"Get on my horse with me, Tress. I'll take you home."

"Thank you, Eloika. Mama's rule is 'Be home before dark.'"

It felt good to think about family rules and to ride behind Eloika with Lucky following and barking now and then. As we approached the cabin, a warm circle of light illumined the ground outside the kitchen window. I no longer felt lonely and friendless. Eloika's needing me to confide in made the difference. I was sure Henry would be all right. And suddenly I knew that I, too, would be all right. I had lost Luke but, like Henry, had my family and many interests in my quiver.

"Mama lighted the lamp for us, Lucky," I said as I slipped off Eloika's pinto.

"Thank you for letting me talk to you, Teresa," she said and galloped away.

Lucky and I made our way out of the trees into the light. I bent down and hugged Lucky once more before we went inside.

"Papa always said to keep your mind busy when your heart is in trouble, Lucky. If there's any hope at all for Mr. Stebbins' school, I'm going to work as hard as I can to help — if he hasn't given up. And . .

and Lucky . . . Sarah can have . . . Luke. I have other arrows in my quiver."

One last tear rolled down my cheek.

Thad sat at the table doing his lessons by lamp-light. I tried to walk by him into the bedroom so that I wouldn't have to talk to him. I was about to close my door.

"Tress," he said. "We haven't asked Papa Willie if we could have a school in his cabin."

I stopped. I turned around. "You're right," I said, "We haven't."

CHAPTER 17

Love According to Henry and Axtel

W E WERE ALL worried about Henry. He seemed lost in thought and uninterested in what was going on around him. He took long walks in the woods by himself without telling anyone where he was going. I often found him sitting on Resting Rock looking blankly out over the river. Mama worried because he didn't come regularly to meals and ate whenever and whatever he pleased and sometimes not at all.

One day in late July as we sat down to supper without him, Mama said, "Teresa, do you remember how you acted the day we came home from the races? Henry is acting the same way, but for a longer spell. You never told me what was wrong. Whatever it was, do you think the same thing might be bothering Henry?

"She was in love," Thad said with a smirk.

"I still am," I said. "I'll never get over missing Luke. I miss his not coming for water. I miss going into Spokane Falls with him with his loads of cordwood. I haven't seen Eloika around lately, maybe Henry is missing her."

"That could be it. Could be Henry's had a falling out with Eloika," Papa Willie said.

"I'll ask him," I said.

"He'll tell you to mind your own business," Thad said.

"I want to get to the bottom of this," Mama said. "Henry should be finishing his high school studies so he can take the state examination."

"I'll have to be giving him more garden chores," Papa Willie said, "so's the outside air will have a chance to work on him. It just ain't like Henry to mope."

"Could be that more outside work would do him some good," Mama agreed. "His studies and building the new room and barn have kept him inside."

The next day I was paring carrots for supper when Henry came in and made himself a sandwich. He took it out to the picnic table. Although I had had lunch, I dried my hands, made a sandwich and followed him out. I sat down beside him. "Henry," I said, "I need some help."

He looked up. "Having trouble with Papa Willie? He keeps a tight ship."

"Nothing like that."

"What, then?" He took a bite of his sandwich.

"Henry, I think I'm in love with Luke."

"You ? Luke?"

I nodded. "But he doesn't like me. He likes Sarah Stebbins."

"You said *likes. Like* and *love* are two different things."

"I can't get Luke out of my mind. Isn't that love? He was always nice to me before he met Sarah. He doesn't know I'm alive now. He never comes for water any more."

"Sarah's ford is right on his way when he comes from town. I never heard him say anything about liking any girl. His cordwood business keeps him busy, Tress. That's probably why he hasn't been here lately. He's too busy. Anyway, there's a big difference between liking and loving."

"How different?"

Henry thought a minute. "You know I want to marry Eloika. I'm in love with her."

"Then why don't you marry her?"

"I didn't get that job at Rathdrum. I would have no way to support her. For me, love is wanting to take care of the one I love. Wanting to provide for her."

"I don't want to take care of Luke or have him taking care of me. I just want to be with him."

"I'm no expert, Tress; but I'd say you really aren't in love with Luke. Back in New York, I liked Honey Smith, remember? And I missed her companionship for a while after we came to the prairie. But that feeling was nothing like I feel for Eloika. I think that was what some people call a crush. I liked Honey, and liked to be with her; but what I feel for Eloika is true love."

"I know she loves you, Henry. She told me so. I think you should get married."

Henry shook his head. "Not until I have a job."

"What about her being half Indian and you not?"

"That doesn't matter to either of us."

"Cash-up Vandersims says there will be jobs for every able bodied man that wants work if he can get Mr. Stebbins to agree to sell his land for the warehouse."

Henry looked at me with interest. "Did he say that?"

"He did."

"I think I'll go into town and talk to Vandersims. If I can get a temporary job at the warehouse that pays enough so I can take care of Eloika, I'll marry her right away."

"Henry, Eloika is moving to DeSmet."

"I know. I'm willing to live there if she will have me."

"If the warehouse comes, Mr. Stebbins says there won't be a school. The people he planned on helping him with the school will get paying jobs at the warehouse. Thad and I want the school *and* the warehouse."

"The school would be best for your future," Henry said. "Most warehouse jobs don't have much future. People don't think much about the future. Thad said he wants to be a geologist. That takes education. How does Luke feel about the school?"

"Even if there is a school, his parents probably won't let him go. He wants the school only so Sarah won't go back to Minnesota."

"How do you feel about Sarah? Do you want her to stay here?"

"No."

"Then why do you want the school?"

"I'm all mixed up, Henry. Thad and I want the

school and the warehouse. If we get the ware-house, we can't have the school. If we get the school, Sarah will stay. I want Sarah to go away so Luke will forget her and visit us like he used to. Oh, I don't know what I want."

"Tress, I'll tell you what I think. I think you've been more lonely than you realize here on the prairie. I know I have. It's easy to think you're in love when you're lonely. With no one in your life your own age but Luke, it's easy to think he's more important to you than he is. Loneliness does funny things to people without their realizing it."

Henry took his empty plate into the house.

"Teresa, Hs-s-t, Teresa," a voice whispered.

I looked behind me. There was no one there.

"Teresa, over here, behind the bushes." The voice was louder.

I got up and walked toward a cluster of thimble-berry bushes.

"Axtel! What are you doing here? Come out of there. Come over to the table. You can have the other half of my sandwich."

"Be quiet, Teresa. I don't want anyone to know I'm here. Walk down the road until you're out of sight of the house. I'll meet you there. Bring the sandwich. I'm starved. Your house is a long walk from Trent. Don't let anyone see me. I have to talk to you."

Puzzled, I followed his instructions. I could hear him moving in the bushes.

Suddenly he stepped out. "This is far enough. No one will see us here. I don't want anyone to know where I am. Teresa, I ran away from home."

"You what?"

"I ran away from home and I'm not going back."

"Why ?"

"Mother and Father are packing. They're going to sell our property to Mr. Vandersims. We're all to go back to Minnesota to get ready for the fall term of school. I want to stay here. This is my kind of life."

"It's only July. Your father should try a little longer to get the school started here."

Why did I say that? I didn't want the school, did I? Oh, I was so mixed up!

"Father says it's no use. He's given up. Mr. Vandersims has everybody believing that the warehouse will be better for the people than a school building. A territorial school would mean higher taxes and Mother will have nothing less."

"That's no reason for you to run away. Your ma is thinking about what's good for your future. You're making more worry for your father. Where will you stay? How will you live?"

"I'm hoping I can stay with you."

"You're what?"

"I'm hoping I can stay in your barn until I figure out what to do. I told Father and Mother how much it means to me to stay here. They don't listen."

"You should help your pa with the school, not run away."

Axtel shook his head. His bushy mop of red hair fell over his eyes. "Father's given up. Will you let me stay here?"

"I'll have to ask Mama and Papa Willie, Axtel."

"Can't I just hide in your barn without them knowing it?"

"Maybe for a few hours, but Thad would soon find you when he goes to feed and groom the horses."

I remembered how horrid I felt when I didn't tell Mama and Papa about going to the railroad bridge. I didn't want any more of that. "If you stay here, I'll have to tell," I said.

"Could I stay with Eddie Chuck in the lean-to barn?"

"That would be up to Eddie. He's the boss of the lean-to. He might let you live with him if your mother and father agree; but I don't think he would hide you. Papa Willie's got him turned around in his thinking from what he used to be."

"There's another reason I want to stay, Teresa."

"You hate school?"

"No, I like school . . . You . . . are . . . fun to be with."

Was Axtel trying to say he had a crush *on me*?

"You hardly know me, Axtel."

"I liked you from the first — when I upset your groceries at the Bridge . . . and you didn't get mad. Let's go see what Eddie Chuck says about keeping me in the lean-to barn."

"Eddie Chuck is in the garden. Papa Willie is there, too. The others are all somewhere in the yard. I won't be able to keep them from seeing you. Instead of finding Eddie, let's find Papa Willie and tell him that you want to stay here and that you don't want to go back to Minnesota. We'll see what he thinks you should do."

"He'll tell me to go back to Minnesota with my family."

"We'll make him promise not to talk to your folks until you say he can."

Reluctantly, Axtel agreed.

CHAPTER 18

Another Hired Hand

Papa WILLIE WAS in the new part of the garden saying goodbye to two old friends. I immediately recognized them as Martin and O'Malley. I nodded to them as they left but didn't waste time with introductions.

"Axtel and I want to talk to you, Papa Willie," I said.

"Can't do it now. Got to get the young carrots, turnips and beets harvested so Thad can take them to the California Hotel tomorrow morning. The extra garden is beginning to pay off. We're in business now, Teresa Girl. Business has to come before pleasure. Talking to me old friends has set me back some."

Papa Willie pulled a bunch of young carrots and held them up for our inspection. Noticing Axtel, he said, "How about you lending a hand, Young Man, if you've got nothing better to do."

"Glad to," Axtel said. "Mr. Whitehouse, seeing as how you seem to need help, could I earn my keep here for a few days?"

"Looking for work, are you? We could use an extra hand harvesting the early crop. Three days, you say?"

"As long as you need me. I could put in a longer work day if I could sleep here during harvest season."

"No extra beds except the one in the new barn. You can have that if your mama and papa say so. I'll be paying you by the work day. If you put in a full day, 75¢ a day."

"The barn will do me for sleeping. Thank you, Mr. Whitehouse."

"What did Martin and O'Malley want, Papa Willie? Were they just visiting?"

"They've been taking care of me place for me. Now they've decided to try their luck in Idaho at the mines. Means I'll either have to put me spread up for sale or rent it out. Bad time of the year for that to come about. Just when I'm needed here with the crops coming on."

He turned to Axtel. "If you turn out to be a good worker, Son, you could free me up here for a spell while I get me own property taken care of."

"I'll do my best, Mr. Whitehouse. I'll get right to work as soon as I walk Teresa to the house."

"I'll show Axtel where the tools are," I said.

At the edge of the garden, Axtel stopped, "Papa Willie thinks I was looking for work, Teresa. Let's leave it that way. Then I won't have to tell your family that I ran away from home."

"What about your mother and father? They'll be worried about you."

"I'll think of something. I'd best get to work now."

"Me, too. I have to help Mama with the ironing."

"Don't tell her I ran away."

"I'll tell her the truth: Uncle Willie hired you to work here for a few days. She'll have to know that or she won't know to put an extra plate out at supper time."

"I want to stay for a long time, Teresa," Axtel said.

I didn't answer.

Mama was happy to know that Axtel would be an extra hand.

"I've been worried that William has been putting too much work on Henry. The boy is certainly not getting any livelier."

"Mama, work isn't what Henry needs. He needs Eloika. He told me so," I said.

"I've been thinking Eloika might have something to do with Henry's trouble. Do you know this for a fact, Teresa?"

"Henry told me," I repeated.

"Thank you for telling me, Teresa."

"I've something else to tell you, Mama," I blurted out. "Axtel isn't just another farm hand. He's run away from home."

"Run away? Does William know that?"

I shook my head.

"We'll have to tell William, Teresa. We'll also have to let the Stebbins know that Axtel is here. Harboring a runaway is something like harboring a criminal."

"Mama, please pretend I didn't tell you. Don't let Axtel know you know. He would never trust me again."

"I'm making no promises, Teresa. I'll at least have to talk to William about this."

"Oh, Mama," I groaned.

She shook me awake early the next morning. The house was quiet.

She spoke softly, trying not to awaken the others. "Teresa, William and I both agree. The Stebbins are probably worried out of their minds about Axtel not coming home last night. You'll have to take Charlie and the cart this morning and tell them that Axtel is here and Papa Willie is willing for him to help with the harvest for the rest of the summer. You will have to go alone. William can't spare the boys today. If you start now, you'll be back by noon and will be able to get in half a days' work. Get dressed."

Now that the addition to the house was built and the extra garden space was established, I helped mostly with indoor chores and seldom wore overalls. I slipped into my dark green long skirt, my white shirtwaist and button shoes and was ready. I liked wearing dresses. Work clothes were too stiff and hard.

"Can't Axtel come with me and explain to his parents, Mama?" I asked.

"No sense. You're old enough now to go alone and deliver the message. William is paying Axtel wages and wants him on the job."

"Suppose Axtel's folks don't want him staying here?"

"You'll have to explain he's hired himself out."

"How will I get across the river?"

"Take Happy and Merry instead of Charlie and put the canoe in the wagon. The river is down to summer level; you'll be able to cross in the canoe. Now, be on your way."

146

Driving the new wagon alone was still a novelty. Dressed up as I was, I felt very independent and grown-up but how I wished Luke was with me. He had once told me that he liked girls in dresses. He would like my green skirt.

As I drove along the Mullan Road and approached the sign on the tree that pointed the way to the Aarons, out of habit I stopped and looked up that trail. What a surprise! Coming down the hill in his wagon loaded with cordwood on his way to Spokane Falls was Luke. I smoothed my hair.

"Luke!" I called. "Luke!"

He reined in his team at the Mullan Road.

"Teresa, what are you doing up so early? Is someone sick?"

I hesitated. Should I tell him about Axtel? I had to. He would know there was some sort of emergency to bring me out alone this early in the morning.

"Good for Axtel," Luke said. "Sarah doesn't want to go back to Minnesota either. Why do the Stebbins put so much stock in book learning?"

"I agree with the Stebbins that book learning is important, Luke," I said. "But, honestly, I don't see how a few months of learning on their own would hurt the Stebbins while their pa is getting a school going. Nella should give Oliver more time."

"What she thinks is all that seems to matter. I think the man should be the head of the family and do the thinking."

"I think families should be run the way Papa Willie runs our family. With a Meeting of the Clan and each of us having a say."

"With a what?"

"With a Meeting of the Clan," I repeated. "At a Meeting of the Clan, everybody has a say."

"The man earns the money and he should decide things," Luke insisted.

I knew Luke well enough to know there was no use arguing with him when he had his mind made up. His notions about how a family should be run were a lot different than mine.

"I can't talk more now, Luke. Papa Willie wants me back by noon. Why don't you ever stop by our place for water?"

"Busy season," he said. "I stop at Sarah's Ford on my way up from town. What's the canoe for, Teresa?"

"So I can get across the river to the Stebbins place."

"Wish I could help you put it in the water but I've got to get as much as I can out of these horses this morning. I have a stop to make before I get to town. I'll be getting on now. Good luck, Teresa."

He tightened the reins.

I watched him go in a cloud of dust.

He said he wished he could help me put the canoe in the water. Did he mean it? He didn't say anything about seeing me soon or about coming for water. He called me *Teresa*, not *Tress*, as though I were a stranger. He knew I liked Tress better.

Don't think of Luke now. You have an important errand to do, Teresa.

I spurred Happy and Merry to a trot. I couldn't get Luke out of my mind even though I was beginning to think maybe Henry was right. *Maybe I really didn't love Luke*. I certainly didn't like a lot of his notions. Maybe I was just lonely. With his notions about how a family should be run, I knew for sure I didn't want him ever taking care of me.

I passed a miner on a pack mule going east. Also several settlers who, I imagined, were headed for the blacksmith or the general store. The early morning stage passed me, too, the one Henry had taken to Rathdrum.

The rising sun, round and red with stored up heat for the day, climbed higher and higher in the sky.

The few miles to the railroad bridge passed quickly. I had a lot to think about. I tethered Happy and Merry to a tree along the river, then walked back to the road hoping to accost a rider to help me unload the canoe and put it in the water.

The rumble of wagon wheels! I watched anxiously as a dray approached. It was . . . it was the Gatley Transport with Freddie Gatley driving a four-horse team.

"Freddie," I screamed and waved, "I need help!"

She drew up immediately.

I told her my story and asked her for help with the canoe.

"Of course I'll help," she bristled. "I wouldn't be in this business if I couldn't handle the likes of a two-man canoe alone. Out of my way."

Frederika Gatley was one strong woman. She had that canoe sitting peacefully in the shallow edge of the water before I could object to her doing the job alone.

LOVE ACCORDING TO TERESA

She dusted off her hands, adjusted her Stetson hat, smoothed her ample deer hide skirt and asked me how Mr. Stebbins' school was coming along.

"It's not. The Stebbins are giving up. They're going back to Minnesota. Seems that Cash-up Vandersims threw a monkey wrench in the plan for the school. He's discouraging settlers from supporting and helping with the school. He promises the settlers jobs working in the warehouse. Without them helping and pledging money, Mr. Stebbins can't get the school going soon enough to please his wife, Nella. It's a big mess, Freddie. Cash-up hopes to buy the Stebbins' land."

"You say Cash-up Vandersims is the one throwing the monkey wrench in the Stebbins' plans for a school? He's putting the almighty dollar before the educating of the young'uns?"

"Seems that way."

"Why, the old goat. I'll be talking to him."

Freddie climbed back into her dray, waved and yelled back,

"You'll hear more from me."

I could see the Stebbins' row boat on the other shore. I paddled straight for it. It was easy going. The snow was melted off the mountains. The river had quieted down for the summer.

I tied the canoe near the row boat and struck out for the Stebbins.

CHAPTER 19

The Big Diamond

IN THE STEBBINS' front yard shaded by the apple tree was a pile of something under a tarpaulin. I lifted one corner.

School desks, a globe, a Bible, an organ, a teacher's desk.

Sarah Stebbins came to the door, her hair in a pony tail. She certainly was pretty, even in work clothes.

"Teresa! What are you doing here so early?"

"I came about Axtel."

"What about Axtel? He didn't come home last night. He had a disagreement with Mother and Father about not wanting to go back to Minnesota. Mother and Father are worried sick. They and the other boys are out looking for him. Do you know where he is?"

I told her all I knew, changing the true story a little. "Axtel came to our farm looking for work," I said. "Papa Willie hired him. No cause to worry. He's fine, sleeping with the animals in our new barn."

"Why didn't he tell Mother and Father where he was going?"

"I guess he thought your ma and pa wouldn't listen to him. Papa Willie put him right to work and it got dark before any of us realized how late it was. Papa and Mama said he shouldn't walk home alone after dark."

"Teresa, I agree with Axtel. I want to stay here the worst way. He and I thought for sure we would be staying. It looked like there would be a school after all. Did you see the things under the tarpaulin? They were donated for Father's school. Students were signed up. Then that Mr. Vandersims came again — talking up the warehouse, with money to pay warehouse wages a week in advance and money to buy our property. Father needs the warehouse job as much as any other settler, but the warehouse can come only if he sells his property. Where would we live and where could he have the school? He planned the school on the river view half of his property, exactly where the warehouse is to be built. Mr. Vandersims suggested he sell just that half, but that would mean no school and you know how Mother feels about that."

"And your father and mother are going back to Minnesota?"

"For this year."

"You will go with them?"

"We'll all go."

"Axtel signed up to help Papa Willie for the summer."

"Mother and Father will have to straighten that out."

"Thad and I have been wanting a school ever since we came," I said. "But it never seems to come about."

"Even Luke was interested in the school. Did you see the teacher's desk under the tarpaulin? He and his father made and donated that."

"They are good carpenters."

Sarah talked on and on about Luke without waiting for me to answer. Her father thought Luke was a good worker. Her mother enjoyed talking to him. All her brothers liked him.

She had no idea how she hurt me every time she said his name.

I told her I had to be going, that Papa Willie expected me by noon, but I would think about her problem.

She walked to the river bank with me and rowed back across the river next to me in my canoe and helped me load the canoe into the wagon. I thanked her and said she was thoughtful.

"Luke is the thoughtful one, Teresa. This is the second time I've crossed the river this morning. I came here earlier to wave to him as he went by on his way to Spokane Falls with his load of wood. He tries to go by at the same time each morning so that we can see each other as our day begins. Sometimes he has time to stop and we talk a while."

So that was why Luke didn't have time to talk to me — why he had "a stop to make" on his way to Spokane Falls.

"It sounds serious, Sarah."

"I think it is," she answered. "I just can't go back to Minnesota and leave Luke."

"If your father started a school, Luke wouldn't go," I said. "He doesn't want to better himself."

"I would do anything to help Father get a school started and it doesn't matter to me whether Luke goes to the school or not. I don't think he needs more schooling. I like him the way he is. He does well cutting cordwood and carpentering."

I didn't want to hear any more about how special Luke was. I told her again that I had to leave. She asked me to visit again before the family left for Minnesota. I thanked her for helping me with the canoe and was about to turn Happy and Merry toward home when she said, "If only there were an old barn or some other place for the school. Isn't there someone who can spare enough land for a school?"

"No one I know of unless . . . Maybe . . . There is someone. Maybe . . . I'll let you know." I picked up the reins and was on my way.

All the way home I thought of the Stebbins and the school, of Sarah and Luke, of Henry and Eloika, and of Axtel whom I had almost forgotten about. There were so many problems. I also thought of the desks and globe and Bible under the tarpaulin.

All of those things were mixed together in my mind but if *my* plan worked, everything would be straightened out. Everything, that is, except Luke and me; and after listening to Sarah talk about Luke, I was sure there was no such thing as Luke and me . . . unless Sarah went back to Minnesota. So many problems.

The minute I got home, I changed into work clothes, gulped my lunch and headed out to the garden to find Papa Willie. He and Axtel were busy harvesting tender young beets for Thad to take into town to sell to the hotels.

I told him I had to talk to him, but he said, "Can't stop working now, Teresa Girl. Best that you dig in, too."

I assured Axtel that Sarah would explain to his parents where he was; and then, as Papa Willie said, I dug in, helping with the beet harvest.

After supper, Papa Willie lighted his corn cob pipe and sat down out front in an old chair next to the wash bench. He liked to watch the sun set. This was the chance I had been waiting for.

I sat down on the bench next to him. "Papa Willie," I said choosing my words very carefully. "I have something to tell you and a favor to ask you. A really big favor."

"Shoot," he said.

I told him the truth about Axtel running away which he said Mama had already told him. I told him about the globe and organ and desks all ready for the school and that I had decided on the way home to ask Freddie Gatley to bring them here.

"Here? What for?" he asked abruptly.

"Papa Willie," I said. "there's a way Thad and I and the Stebbins could have a school by September if you will do us a favor."

"I already offered my services to the Stebbins," he said,

"This isn't services, Papa Willie."

"What then?"

"Papa Willie, could we start a school in your cabin?"

"In my cabin? It's not fit for man nor beast right now, let alone a school," he said.

"I know, Papa. But Thad and I and the Stebbins boys and Sarah will clean it up. We won't ask you to do a thing. Just let us use your cabin. And not forever. Just until we find a permanent place for the school."

I explained to Papa Willie that if he would donate his cabin, Mr. Stebbins could sell just the river half of his property, where the school was supposed to be, to the warehouse company; and the settlers would be able to have the warehouse *and a school.* I talked mighty hard and fast.

"It will solve everybody's problems," I said.

"Who's everybody?"

"The Stebbins will be able to stay because Thad and the boys and Sarah and I can get your cabin ready for school by September."

I didn't say anything to him about Luke and me. Our problems wouldn't be solved. But if everyone else was happy, I knew that somehow my problem with Luke would work out, too.

"When your cabin is all slicked up, Papa Willie, we'll celebrate by having a big dance and box social to raise money to pay the teacher and pay for books and supplies. The Stebbins boys will play music. Isn't it exciting, Papa Willie?"

"You're going to do all that just when harvest is starting?"

"Yes, Papa, yes," I shrieked, liking the idea more and more the longer I talked. "Your cabin is just sitting there, Papa Willie, with nobody living in it and all those injured animals needing to be cared for. If you would let us use it for a school, I promise to see to watering and feeding the critters."

"Teresa," Papa Willie said, "that sounds like a mighty wild scheme to me. Bears a lot of thought."

"Papa, there isn't time for thinking. The settlers are going to take back their donations. The Stebbins are packing to go back to Minnesota. I've got to talk to Freddie Gatley tomorrow and get her to get Cash-up to help us instead of being against us. Even if I have to work in the harvest every Sunday for the rest of the month, I'll have to have tomorrow off."

"I'll run all this over with your mama. Sounds to me like this calls for a Meetin' of the Clan."

"That takes too long, Papa Willie. Can't we get everybody together right now down at Emmy's Grove and decide?"

Papa Willie didn't have time to answer. Wagon wheels were coming up our hill.

"Who would be coming this time o' day?" he asked.

It was FRED GATLEY'S TRANSPORT AND STORAGE COMPANY. Sitting as smart as you please beside Frederika Gatley on the driver's seat was none other than Cash-up Vandersims, hair slicked back, collar starched and leather brief case on his lap. Beside him was an old gentleman who was a dead ringer for Freddie.

"Must be Freddie's daddy," Thad said.

"You expecting a delivery?" Papa Willie asked me.

"No." I was as bewildered as he was.

Mama, Emmy, Henry, Eddie Chuck, Axtel and Lucky gathered around to see what FRED GATLEY'S TRANSPORT AND STORAGE was doing in our yard.

"You got some unloading to do here?" Papa Willie asked Freddie as she bounded down from the driver's seat. I was surprised to see that she was dressed in a wide flowered skirt and white shirt-waist and the wisps of her hair that usually flew about her face were neatly caught up in two fancy combs on either side of her head. Freddie was dressed up!

"I've come for my map," Cash-up said as he climbed out of the wagon and stood beside Freddie. "But first, Freddie has an announcement." He was his usual business-like self.

Freddie held out her left hand. Her gnarled ring finger sparkled with a gold wedding band and next to it, the biggest solitaire diamond I had ever seen. I didn't know whether or not the diamond was real. I didn't know diamonds well enough to decide about that. But I did know that the wedding band was real and the diamond was big.

In her equally big voice, ringing with happiness, Fredericka Wilhelmina Gatley announced, "My name is now Mrs. Elliot Vandersims and this here is my husband, Elliot Vandersims."

The tone of her voice when she said *Elliot* made it plain that from now on, no one was to call her husband *Cash-up*.

"The name of this here business, as soon as Elliot changes the lettering on the dray, from then on is GATLEY AND VANDERSIMS TRANSPORT, STORAGE AND REALTY. This here's now a joint venture with me, my daddy and Mr. Elliot Vandersims, the only men I know that I would ever consider teaming up with."

She pointed proudly to Elliot and then to the old gentleman beaming in the wagon. "This here's my daddy. He's riding with Elliot and me for a spell till he's sure Elliot's got a handle on this transport business. When Daddy says Elliot is one hundred percent ready to take over, I'm figuring on staying home and learning to cook. Daddy's put in for grandchildren."

The old gentleman in the wagon did not stop beaming.

The rest of us were too surprised at the turn of events to do or say much more than, " Congratulations, Mr. and Mrs. Vandersims," and then stare at the unlikely couple.

"I'll get the map," finally Thad said and ran into the house.

CHAPTER 20

Everything Settled
(Almost)

I HAD HANDED the map to Elliot Vandersims who spread it out on the picnic table.

Taking Freddie's hand again and in his most dignified, business-like voice with a glance now and then at Daddy Gatley in the wagon to make sure he approved, Elliot said, "I don't have to tell you that this map shows the warehouse my client hopes to build not far from Plante's Ferry. You also know that Mr. Stebbins legally bought that property last year; but because of a mix-up at the courthouse, the sale was not entered into the records. My client subsequently bought the same piece of property and went ahead with plans for the warehouse."

"Elliot, tell them how you and me have undertaken to untangle this unholy mix-up," Freddie said.

"To begin with, this community needs the jobs the warehouse will bring. Mr. Stebbins, himself, needs a job there. He also needs the home he has built on the property. I have been able to show both Mr. Stebbins and my client that they need to work together. They now are willing to compromise. Mr. Stebbins will keep the half of the prop-

161

erty he built his home on. My client will keep the half of the property along the river and will build the warehouse there as planned. Each will be reimbursed for the half paid for but no longer owned."

That was almost the way I had figured that the tangle could be untangled.

One person was still unhappy: "That won't stop Mother and Father from taking us back to Minnesota," Axtel said. "There still won't be a school."

"Just a minute, Young Fella," Freddie said. "My agreement to marry Elliot Vandersims was brought about by more than him giving me this ring." Freddie held out her left hand again, turning it this way and that so the diamond reflected the light.

Elliot interrupted, "Freddie and her daddy bought the piece of land next to the Stebbins. They're dividing it into ten-acre tracts that I'm to sell to the new settlers who'll be coming to work at the warehouse. . ."

Freddie interrupted, "I made it plain to Elliot that no development will be worth a tinker's damn without a piece of land set aside for a school building. And seeings as how I've been bringing Elliot a lot of business, letting him know who the new folks are in town, I said,

"'Cash-up Vandersims,' (I called him Cash-up in them days) 'it's up to you to buy ten acres of my and my daddy's newly purchased property and donate it for a school.'

"Elliot done what I said without batting an eyelash. Him and me wants you folks to know that ten acres of prime property right next to the Stebbins' property is set aside on county records for the first school building down Plante's Ferry way. So, you see, Young Fella, there *is* a school in the making.

"Elliot, mark it off on that map so Axtel and Thad and Teresa will know where the school will be and that it is all legal-like," Freddie finished.

Elliot marked it off.

"Now everything's settled," Freddie said. She took the map that now showed the school, rolled it in the oil cloth, secured it with the leather strap and stuck it in the belt of her ample skirt. "I'll be keeping this map, Elliot Vandersims, just so there's no change of plans. Get yourself back in the wagon and we'll be on our way."

Cash-up and Freddie, excuse me, Mr. and Mrs. Vandersims climbed aboard. Sitting as straight and grand as when she came, she turned the team and wagon around and headed down our hill.

Soon we saw dust rising above the trees on the Mullan Road westward and knew that Freddie, her new husband and daddy were headed home.

Axtel Stebbins was the only one who looked sad. "The school won't be ready in time for us," he said. "We'll still have to go back to Minnesota."

Papa Willie looked at him thoughtfully. "You're a mighty fine hand, Axtel, Me Lad. Guess it's me turn to have a say in these goings-on."

What had Papa Willie decided? Was he going to let us use his cabin for a school?

Mama turned to go inside.

"Don't nobody leave," Papa Willie said. "I'm calling a Meeting of the Clan here and now. It don't matter that it ain't breakfast time or that Thad does-n't have his harmonica and I don't have me drum. There's a heap of deciding to do."

"Are you going to let us use your cabin for a tem-porary school, Papa Willie?" I asked.

"Just keep your britches on, Teresa Girl." He turned toward Axtel. "If your mama is so set on hav-ing a school by September, there's a chance it can come to pass. Me cabin's vacant and me animals need watering and feeding. Teresa is willing to take over that job, but it will take more than just her to turn the place into a school."

"I know what you're going to say, Papa," Thad said. "You're going to want to know if we all are willing to help make the school come about. I know I'm ready to help. I'll even work evenings to get your place ready for school by September."

"So will I." "Me, too." There was a chorus of agreement with Emmy as loud as the rest.

"All us Stebbins will help, too," Axtel said.

"That sounds like a vote in favor of the school to me," Papa Willie said. "Here and now I'm a-putting Thad in charge of the work party to make sure every member of both families put their shoulders to the wheel and get this school going. And on opening day, Thad, you're to see to it that the county superintendent is here to see what's going on. I want everybody who plans on going to me school to get a good look at a real superintendent."

"You said, '*my* school', Papa Willie."

"That's because the new school will be named the William Webster Whitehouse Territorial

School. And Thad, instead of studying your books tonight, you take that split log over there and letter them words on it. We'll hang it over the doorway where every pupil will know that the territory is backing me new school."

Oh joy! Everything was turning out right. Everything, that is, except Luke and me. He had always been a part of our celebrations. It was hard to erase thoughts of Luke.

"And, Axtel, at the first crack of dawn, you are to take Charlie and the cart and tell your pa and ma to start unpacking, that you and your brothers and Teresa and Thad will have a school building ready by September. Me good wife, Addy, already ordered books for her family so she knows about that. We'll put her in charge of the book getting. Tell your papa to go on with filing papers with the county."

"Can Teresa come with me, Mr. Whitehouse?"

"What do you say, Teresa Girl?"

"Oh, yes, Papa Willie, yes. I will need Sarah to help me with a basket social to pay for the school books and to pay the teacher. Papa Willie, Axtel and I will need the wagon to carry the canoe so we can get across the river."

"And, Thad, while you're lettering the sign that says *William Webster Whitehouse Territorial School*, we'll need a notice to post at the Bridge announcing the basket social. And, Teresa Girl, when you get to Axtel's house, tell Mr. Stebbins to get the fiddlers practiced up for playing dance music at the social."

"Yes, Papa Willie."

Papa Willie was as excited about the doings as the rest of us. He never said a word to Axtel and me about making up work time on the week-end because we were taking time off to go to the Stebbins.

We carried out his instructions exactly.

In the morning when Axtel and I got to the place on the Mullan Road where *Aaron* was lettered on a sign shaped like an arrow, I completely forgot to look up the trail for Luke. (How could I have forgotten that?)

Then I heard a shout,

"Teresa!"

166

There he was, coming down the trail with his cordwood.

I waved and felt a sudden twinge of joy that he had called to me.

"We better not wait for him," Axtel said. "Papa Willie said not to dawdle." Axtel spurred Merry and Happy to a trot.

Once in a while I looked back to see how close Luke was, but soon we had far outdistanced him with his heavily loaded wagon.

He caught up to us as we were unloading the canoe.

I waved to him, but he didn't stop to talk to me.

CHAPTER 21

Luke Aaron Arrives

THE STEBBINS WERE overjoyed that the property dilemma was settled. Mr. Stebbins could keep his home and had a job to his liking at the warehouse, and it looked like Papa Willie had made possible the organizing of a school by September.

At a Meeting of the Clan, it was decided that the box social and dance would be held on the first Saturday in September, that guests would arrive about four o'clock, and we would auction off the baskets at the supper hour. Thad with his harmonica and the Stebbins boys, well known since the parade as The Fiddlers Four, would supply the music.

Lucky for us, Papa's cabin was all one 12' x 16' room, just about the size of many territorial schools at that time. It would be big enough for our dance if everyone didn't dance at once. Since Valley weather could be counted on to be nice in September, the box social would be held outside.

Papa Willie donated his table (that had been our picnic table since the quarantine). Outside under a tree, it would hold the gaily decorated baskets to be auctioned one by one.

How we ever got the garden work done and Papa Willie's cabin cleaned and decorated and the O.K. from the Territorial Superintendent all by September, I'll never know.

No, that's wrong. I do know. It was work, work, work from early morning until late at night and the help of neighbor settlers that made everything happen as planned. The neighbors, hearing at the Bridge what we were trying to do, worked right along with us whenever they could spare a day in exchange for promise of an invitation to the Dedication, Box Social and Dance.

Fredericka Gatley Vandersims and Elliot worked hard, too. In their dray they brought the table-like desks and benches and other donated school equipment from the Stebbins' yard to Papa Willie's cabin as soon as Papa said we Wickstroms and the Stebbinses had made it "fit for human habitation."

In Papa's language that meant the prairie grasses on the immediate acre were scythed, the building was totally cleaned and the floor smoothed off as much as possible for dancing.

When September actually rolled around, most of the school equipment was still under a tarpaulin in what we now called the "schoolhouse yard." The exceptions were kerosene lamps that hung on the walls to light the schoolroom and the school benches along the walls for weary dancers or dance onlookers.

Although Mrs. Stebbins insisted, "Those boys need to get to their studies," and wanted school to start immediately after it was dedicated, the first day was set for mid-September.

Amidst all the cleaning and spiffing up, the Stebbins were building something mysterious in the school yard. It had two uprights connected by a cross-bar. Axtel assured me that "it was something everybody would like."

"When can we know what it is?" I asked.

"At the school dedication."

Not even Thad could guess what it was.

As September approached and construction progressed, when the Stebbins finished working each day on the mystery object, they wrapped it in burlap. We talked about it and guessed but still could not imagine what was under the wrappings.

About a week before the Box Social, a horseman from the County School Superintendent's office arrived to say that Superintendent McMahan would be pleased to attend dedication ceremonies but that, unfortunately at the moment, we were lacking three students if we hoped to receive enough state funds to pay the twenty-five-dollars-a-month teacher's salary.

I wanted to sign up Luke, but as I feared, his father was adamant: "Luke already knew all he needed to know."

Freddie, Eddie Chuck and Papa Willie solved the enrollment problem by letting us sign them up, saying they would attend the school when work permitted. Fortunately, ages were not required on the attendance roster.

"But who was the new teacher?"

None of us knew.

The Stebbins boys practiced their fiddling and Thad his harmonica until they could play together with their eyes closed "Turkey in the Straw", "She'll Be Comin' Round the Mountain", "Oh! Dem Golden Slippers", and "Little Brown Jug".

At the last minute, Papa Willie decided his small cook stove should be left in the room to warm the school children on cold days and so that there would be a place to bake the potatoes pioneer children often brought for their lunches.

"You don't know but what a cold spell will come before Mr. Stebbins has the real school built and going," Papa Willie said.

We were afraid the fiddle music would unsettle the injured raccoon, squirrel and baby robin Papa Willie had been nursing back to health so Freddie and Cash-up moved the animal pens behind a stand of young alders. Near there we had built an extra outhouse so there would be one for boys and one for girls.

At ten o'clock the first Saturday in September Henry securely nailed over the schoolhouse door the split log announcing that this was the William Webster Whitehouse Territorial School. Papa Willie's Civil War flag flew from a home-made flag pole in the front yard.

Although the festivities were not to begin until four, at one o'clock the hitching posts at the side of the school were filled. Decorated baskets covered Papa Willie's table when Cash-up Vandersims, wearing his Prince Albert coat in spite of the heat, brought the largest basket I had ever seen.

"Freddie's," he said. "She made enough for the superintendent, too. That sprig of wild purple

daisies around the handle is so I won't forget which basket is hers."

Completely caught up in the holiday spirit, he happily flapped the tails of his coat, and strode off.

I decorated my basket with pheasant feathers. Axtel often brought me pretty ones he found in the garden. I had saved them.

Papa Willie looked wonderfully elegant in a vest and red sleeve garters and starched white collar tied with a black string tie. His watch chain dangled at his waist.

When Elliot Vandersims seemed to assume that he would be auctioneer, Willie quickly suggested that he should greet the guests and show them around the grounds since, being a real estate sales-man, people were his field of expertise.

Cash-up agreed saying, "Good idea. Meeting peo-ple is my day-to-day job. Could be I'll meet some folks not happily situated who are anxious to invest in the new development.

He carried a plat map. Now and then I spied him sitting on a bench in the schoolhouse with his map stretched out, explaining to a guest where the per-manent school would be and that the "few remain-ing lots were a steal at only six dollars and fifty cents an acre." (Railroad price was $5 an acre.)

By four o'clock he had sold four choice lots.

In exchange for Papa Willie giving him the job of greeter, Cash-up made sure all the guests read the sign over the schoolhouse door. Then he pointed out Papa Willie, the celebrity for whom the school was named.

"That gentleman made all this possible by donat-ing *temporarily* this piece of property for the school," he told everyone, emphasizing the word *temporarily.* He added without humility, that he, Elliot Vandersims and his wife Freddie Gatley Van-dersims had donated the land on which the *per-manent* school would be built.

When one guest asked if the permanent school would be named for him and Freddie, Cash-up smiled knowingly, "Only time will tell, but it seems likely."

He also pointed out Mrs. William Webster White-house dressed in her "Betsy Ross dress" of cabin moving fame. "She is the author of the school motto hanging on the north wall, lettered by her son, Thaddeus."

The guests read with head nodding approval:

3 D's to Success
Desire
Discipline
Dedication

In September along the roads and trails of Northwood Prairie, wild purple daisies bloomed in profusion. Abraham Stebbins and Emmy picked a bucketful and, standing side by side near the doorway of the schoolhouse, presented one to each of the lady guests.

When Freddie told Mr. Stebbins that all the guests were present, he rounded up Thad and The Fiddlers Four in their matching plaid shirts and overalls and the music began. The surrounding woods and hills echoed the joyous sounds. The adult guests immediately ambled two by two into the schoolhouse and the dance floor creaked and crackled, also joyously, under the scuffing of boots and button shoes.

My job was to watch over the picnic baskets until the raffle started. I thrilled when I saw Luke Aaron and his ma and pa arrive in Luke's wagon. I hadn't been sure they would come. Liza Aaron brought Mama a red rose from her garden that exactly matched the trimming on Mama's dress.

After he cared for his horses, Luke walked toward me. *Was he going to ask which basket was mine?*

"Do you know where Sarah is, Teresa?"

I pointed her out under a tree, in charge of the
punch bowl, and not knowing what else to say, I
asked, "Do you want to know which basket is
hers?"

"I already know," he said confidently and walked
in her direction. I knew then that he wouldn't be
bidding on my basket.

CHAPTER 22

The Box Social

PARTIES ON THE prairie usually ended in a story telling contest, the winner's prize being the remains of the party cake. Since this was a box social, there was no cake and there would be a dance instead of a story telling contest. Therefore, Papa Willie would not be telling a story as usual.

Instead, he selected himself to be Master of Ceremonies and Auctioneer. He parked Mabel and his cart not far from the Stebbins' secret project, telling everyone that his cart would be the stage.

As supper time approached, he stopped the music of the Fiddlers Four and announced to the dancers that the dedication ceremonies were about to begin.

Just as he climbed onto the floor of the cart, a woman on horseback dashed into the school yard, her shoulder-length blond hair flying.

"I hope I'm not late," she said as she slid from her saddle. She pushed her hair off her face, smoothed her striped shirtwaist and riding skirt and took Willie's extended hand as he pulled her onto the platform beside him.

The stage wobbled dangerously and Willie said, "Best to set yourself down and rest."

The guests, speculating on who the lady could

be, gathered around Papa Willie's cart. All eyes were on the new arrival.

"Who is she?"

"Never seen 'er before."

In spite of his unsteady platform, Willie stood secure and proud.

In a loud voice that carried into the schoolhouse, he announced, "This here's Rosa McMahan, the county superintendent of schools, come for the dedication."

The tall, slender middle-aged woman stood up and the cart wobbled again, "Most happy to be invited to the dedication of your new school-house," Mrs. McMahan said.

Everyone applauded amidst comments such as, "A woman superintendent?" "Never heard tell of such a thing." Mama herself exclaimed rather loudly, "Well, I never."

Noticing the surprise of the audience and hearing the audible comments, the superintendent said quietly, "Times are changing, you know," and smiled. The comments ceased. She added, "Don't let me interrupt. Go on with your program."

Freddie nudged Cash-up. "You're the greeter. Do your job. Make her welcome."

Cash-up smoothed his hair, approached the cart and held out his hand. "Elliot Vandersims, Dealer in Land, Mrs. McMahan. We are proud that you could come. I am at your service during these goings-on."

Rosa McMahan shook his outstretched hand and smiled again.

Papa Willie, swaying now and then to keep his balance on the wobbly cart floor and somewhat overcome by being in the presence of a superintendent, called unsteadily, "The ceremony will now begin. All gather 'round the Stebbins' secret project."

We would finally see what was under the burlap.

Oliver and Nella Stebbins ripped the wrappings from the secret project.

Exclamations of delight erupted from the crowd and then a burst of applause.

From the cross bar between the two upright posts hung a silver-colored bell somewhat like one I had seen on a fire wagon in the parade.

"Ring it. Ring it," the crowd shouted.

"Mrs. McMahan, it would please me to have you ring the bell here and now so the young'uns will hear what it sounds like to be called to a real school by a real school bell," Papa Willie said.

"Oliver's Grandpa Stebbins brought this bell from England," Nella announced to the crowd. She handed the end of the dangling bell cord to Mrs. McMahan. Mrs. McMahan pulled the bell clapper toward her. It struck the side of the bell. Echoes of the clang reverberated through the hills as though a distant fire wagon were rushing to a fire.

The crowd listened, transfixed, until Superintendent McMahan announced in a voice as clear as the bell, "I hereby dedicate the William Webster Whitehouse Territorial School," and pulled the cord again.

When the mixture of bell echoes and applause died down, the superintendent moved again toward Willie's cart. The crowd followed her.

Again, with Cash-up's hand to help, she climbed onto the stage. "It is now my pleasure to introduce the person who will teach the students of the William Webster Whitehouse School."

"A teacher!" "Didn't know a teacher was hired." "Who is it?" the crowd murmured and looked around expectantly.

There were no strangers in the group.

Then HENRY made his way through the crowd and stood proudly beside Willie and the superintendent in the rickety cart.

She continued, "I am pleased to announce that Henry Wickstrom passed the state examination last week and has been hired by Mr. and Mrs. Elliot Vandersims as teacher. The Vandersims have paid Mr. Wickstrom's first month's salary."

Again the cool evening air sounded with applause and shouts of approval. Henry, looking very professional in his pin-striped vest and trousers to match, announced that he would try to do his best. He swung off Willie's cart backwards amidst a hail of congratulations and back slaps.

Winding her way to his side came Eloika in a hand-beaded dress of white deerskin. Her jet black hair flowed over her shoulders. She kissed Henry and led him toward the bench where she had been sitting.

As they passed me, I whispered to Henry, "Now, you'll marry Eloika, won't you?"

"Teresa," Henry reprimanded, "this is no place to discuss that."

Already I was in trouble with my teacher.

Mama, standing next to me smiled happily and affirmed, "They're going to be married."

"Will Henry move to DeSmet?"

"We'll live wherever Henry's work takes him," Eloika said.

Henry would be my teacher! Eloika would be my sister! Oh, joy! In spite of Henry's scowl, I raced after them, threw my arms around Henry, then Eloika, kissed each of them and said, "I'm so glad. I'm so glad."

The news of Henry's and Eloika's pending marriage trickled through the crowd. The box social took on the air of a party and the party-goers, led by Papa Willie, moved toward the punch table where Sarah stood. "A round of punch for everyone," Papa said. "I propose a toast to Henry Wickstrom and Eloika Tall Spirit. Here's to a long, happy life together."

The Fiddlers Four strode through the yard laughingly playing "Here Comes the Bride". Axtel borrowed a man's large white handerchief and put it over his head like a bridal veil. The audience clapped. Everyone seemed to be having such fun.

"That Axtel is a pistol," Papa Willie said.

The fiddlers brought benches from the schoolhouse and placed them in shady spots around the yard. Axtel pulled me down on one beside him. Oh, this was a happy party.

Superintendent McMahan rang the bell again and Papa announced that the auction was about to begin.

The crowd moved toward the table loaded with decorated lunch baskets. I stayed by Axtel.

Cash-up Vandersims stood close to Papa Willie holding an empty lard tin. Each time Papa sang out, "Going, Going, GONE!", Freddie took the basket to the "lucky young man", accepted the money and handed it to Cash-up who dropped it with a flourish and jangle into the can.

It seemed that all the right people bought all the right baskets; for there was nothing but clapping and good natured shouting and kissing and hugging as each buyer claimed not only the basket but the "pretty young lady" (Papa Willie's words) who had packed the basket.

Henry, of course, got Eloika's without any competition. Cash-up bought Freddie's and they were "delighted to share it with the superintendent." Mr. Stebbins bought Mrs. Stebbins' and shared it with Thad, Asa and Avery.

Papa Willie must have hidden Mama's till last because it didn't appear until he was sure every man, woman and child was part of a small group licking their fingers and exploring such delights as roast prairie hen, beans boiled in oil and red pepper, boiled corn, tomatoes, grapes, apple pie, nougat candy, and raisins.

Papa and Mama shared their basket with Eddie Chuck, Emmy and Abraham. For the first time since we came to the prairie, Emmy had a friend. I was so glad.

Of course, Luke had to keep raising his bid to get pretty Sarah's basket, but he finally got it although he had to borrow a Silver Eagle from his parents to help pay for it. That left Axtel to outbid a boy I didn't know for mine.

Jangling the money in the lard can, Cashup announced proudly as though he alone had earned it, "There's enough money in here to pay all the outstanding debts of the William Webster Whitehouse School. That's what I like to see, cash up front."

When the guests had finished their suppers, Thad and the Fiddlers Four (minus Axtel) started playing "Turkey in the straw". The dancers ambled back inside the schoolhouse.

I began packing the remains of the contents of my basket, when Axtel said to me, "Teresa, do you know what I'd like to do more than anything?"

"What?"

"I'd like to take you for a ride in your canoe."

"You're supposed to be fiddling."

"They don't need me."

"The canoe is turned over on our beach," I answered.

"I'll walk you toward home along the Mullan Road and when we get to your trail, we'll go down toward the river. We can rest at Resting Rock if you want to, and then head for the beach."

"I'll have to tell Mama."

"I'll go with you to tell her."

I was surprised. All Mama said was, "The river is low enough, there's no danger. Stay in the area of our cove and when you hear no more music, start home." She turned to Axtel, "Aren't you supposed to be helping the fiddlers?"

"They can get along without me. Avery is the one who would be missed."

Elliot Vandersims tapped Mama on the shoulder and asked her to dance.

"Run along," she said to us. "Have a good time and don't stay too late."

Mama was having a good time in her Betsy Ross dress.

Mama and Papa liked Axtel. He was a hard worker and had proved himself responsible on the farm. Papa and Eddie Chuck had given him permission to live in the new barn and work after school and on week-ends. When cold weather came and the school term ended, Axtel would go home to his parents.

As he and I walked hand in hand along the trail toward the Mullan Road, we passed Sarah and Luke walking hand in hand. I hardly noticed them. I had found a nice new arrow for my quiver.

The canoe was where I was sure it would be. We turned it over and pushed it off shore into the now quiet, slow running Spokane River. Axtel paddled and I sat in the bow facing him. We could hear the fiddle music drifting through the tall pine trees on the northern shore.

As the canoe moved lazily along, I looked at the sky.

"Axtel, the evening star is out."

A paddle dipped into the water.

"Make a wish, Tress."

"I already did."

"What did you wish?"

"That the warehouse and Papa's temporary school and your father's permanent school will work out and that you Stebbins will stay here on Northwest Prairie forever and ever. What did you wish for, Axtel?"

"I didn't. I'm completely happy right now, Tress. I have nothing more to wish for."

Our eyes met in the dusky light. At that moment I couldn't have wished either. Like Axtel, I had nothing more to wish for.

Book 4 tells of the adventures of Teresa and Thad with the steamboats on Coeur d'Alene Lake.

About the Author

As a teen-ager, Florence Boutwell attended Penn-sauken Junior High and Merchantville High schools located in a suburb of Camden, New Jersey on the Jersey side of the Delaware River.

She looked forward to exploring Pennsylvania on the other side of the river, just as Teresa and Thad look forward to exploring the other side of the Spokane River.

In the 1920s and early '30s, ferry boats docked along the Delaware and carried freight, cars and passengers across the river. Later, the Delaware River Bridge was built, connecting Camden, New Jersey, and Philadelphia, Pennsylvania.

Florence remembers the fun of watching from the deck of a ferry boat, as the deck hands loosed the thick rope moorings when the boat was ready to leave the dock; and later, the thrill of driving across the wonderful awesome new bridge.

In the summer her family lived on Long Beach Island, New Jersey, "six miles at sea". There, she roamed the sand dunes and cattail swamps of the island just as Teresa and Thad roam the trails and hills of Northwood Prairie.

Long Beach Island schoolhouse was a two-story eight-room, red brick structure. Florence imagined how exciting it would be to be the daughter of one of the island fishermen and go to that school within sound of the breaking ocean waves.

But every Fall, her family piled into their Franklin car with the pointed wind shield and headed back to the city.

About the Illustrator

J ANET IVIE was born in Dillon, Montana, and was raised in Conrad, Montana. She earned a Bachelor of Music with a minor in Art, and a Masters of Music Education at the University of Montana, Missoula. For 34 years she taught in Montana and Oregon, the first two years in rural schools followed by music in all grades, kindergarten through college. While teaching music, she continued to study art, emphasizing watercolor and drawing.

Janet is a member of the Watercolor Society of Oregon, the Art Society of Eastern Washington and the Spokane Watercolor Society. Her drawings and paintings have been shown in galleries in Oregon, Washington, Nevada, California and Montana, winning many awards.

She and her husband, Charles, are retired and live in the Spokane Valley where she has a watercolor and drawing studio.

The cover design is water color and pen and ink.

188

Historical Background

MANY READERS have asked me exactly where in the Valley the Wickstrom's lived. Because the family is fictitious, the exact location of their home is also fictitious although, in my mind, I always see them in the hills north of Trentwood.

The location of the temporary school (Willie's cabin) I also see north of Trentwood. That location fits nicely into factual history because it is believed that Trentwood actually was the location of the first, or at least one of the first, schools in the Valley. The problems my characters face while trying to get their school approved for government tax dollars were not unusual.

During the 1880s there was an influx of settlers into the area called Trent. Private schools were starting up and church was being held in Valley homes. By 1887, the date of my story, the growth was noticeable. The area had been platted and was considered briefly as a contender with Spokane Bridge and Spokane Falls for leadership of the larger area that eventually became Spokane. The ferry at Plante's had disappeared by 1860.

The Northern Pacific railroad bridge, built in 1881, crossed the river at Trent, not far from the site of the old Plante's Ferry where a store and boarding house had been built for ferry users. To my knowledge there never was a warehouse there.

In the early days at Spokane Falls, every Fourth of July celebration included horse races. My story of the sleepy-eyed gelding is reported to have actually happened in 1883. (*Saga of a Western Town, Spokane* by Jay Kalez, p.26, Lawton Printing, 1972)

The method Thad used to water his garden (bringing water from his stream in ditches) was widely used after 1900 in many parts of the Valley. For example, in 1901 sixteen miles of main and branch ditches brought small amounts of water from Liberty Lake to 560 acres offered for sale in Greenacres. That method of irrigating the Valley continued for many years.

In my story, Eddie Chuck tells Teresa and Thad stories about Circling Raven. Circling Raven is said to have been an "upright and honest" chief of the Coeur d'Alenes from 1660 to 1760. He was believed to have the gift of prophecy. For more about him, read *Saga of the Coeur d'Alene Indians*, edited by Edward Kowrach and Thomas Connolly, published by Ye Galleon Press, 1990.

Although Lewis and Clark used dug-out canoes, Jerome Peltier in *Manners and Customs of the Coeur d'Alene Indians* (Peltier Publications, 1975, p. 40-41) writes as follows quoting a man who saw an Indian canoe while fishing: ". . . the bark covering the skeleton of the canoe was of mixed white, red and gray birch and lay in patches . . . stuck tight with pitch from the forest . . ."

Much of my information about the procedure for starting a territorial school was gleaned from *Early Schools of Washington Territory* by Angie Burt Bowden, published by Lowman and Hanford Company, Seattle, Washington, 1935